I0646467

FICTION: 12

On the Edge: Three Women

By Feyza Altun

Copyright © 2025 Transnational Press London

All rights reserved. This book or any portion thereof may not be reproduced or used in any manner whatsoever without the express written permission of the publisher except for the use of brief quotations in a book review or scholarly journal.

First published in 2025 by Transnational Press London in the United Kingdom, 21 Woodville Drive, Sale, M33 6NF, UK.
www.tplondon.com

Turkish original version of this book was published by İnkılâp Kitabevi Yayın Sanayi ve Ticaret AŞ, Istanbul, 2024

Transnational Press London® and the logo and its affiliated brands are registered trademarks.

Requests for permission to reproduce material from this work should be sent to: sales@tplondon.com

ISBN: 978-1-80135-203-1 (Paperback)
ISBN: 978-1-80135-337-3 (Digital)

Transnational Press London Ltd. is a company registered in England and Wales No. 8771684.

On the Edge
Three Women

Feyza Altun

TRANSNATIONAL PRESS LONDON
2025

I thank the little girl who travelled with me.
Without you, I couldn't have come here.

Feyza
Kadıköy, November 2019

ABOUT THE AUTHOR

Feyza Altun was born in Üsküdar in 1987. She is a graduate of Marmara University Faculty of Law. She practices law at Altun Law & Consulting. She speaks English, French, and Persian. She currently continues association efforts as the founder of the Neutral Working Mothers Platform. She founded the Women's Union and tries to ensure that women of all views organize for their rights. Altun is the author of the books *Kadının Fenni*, *Kadının Derdi*, and *Kadının Erki*.

feyzaltn@hotmail.com

instagram: @feyzalt

twitter: @feyzaltun

Contents

FOREWORD

There are novels that enter your life; from the very first step, they draw you in and you are captivated by their magic. They make you the person you want to be. They do good for a person; they are a break from the realities of life. The novels where we embody the unforgettable personalities of the Romantics' unforgettable heroes are of this kind. In these novels, we reunite with our loves, we take revenge on the villains.

There are some novels that take us on a journey through the subconscious of a novelist's mind. Their associations may perhaps guide our lives, perhaps give hope... It is exciting to wander through the corridor of these ideas that have not seen the light of day, open to surprises. The mysterious novels of Modernism are of this kind.

Some novels are written for style. The author has created a unique language within the language. You see a thousand different ways of expressing emotion and thought. You see what treasures the language you thought you spoke actually hides, how wide its boundaries are. It takes linguistic skill and elevates it to the skies. The great realist writers of the classics are like this.

There are also some novels that slap us in the face like a blow with the realities we don't want to talk about, that we are afraid to see... A weight collapses on you like a mountain. You can't swallow the bite in your mouth. These are authors stripped of mercy towards the reader, like Emile Zola and the naturalists. But this mercilessness of the author is also the beginning of the birth of a societal mercy. Societal blindness begins to disappear with such novels. You confront evil and arm yourself against it.

Well, Feyza Altun's novel is such a novel. From the first pages, my throat began to tighten. This was the result of stating the truths so nakedly and so simply. Whose truths they are isn't very important, but they are our society's truths.

The neighbour across the street, our distant relatives, the shopkeeper we buy from, a celebrity we admire... What does it matter, they're ours. When I first read the novel, I noticed that Feyza Altun has been fair to every character in her novel. She has almost apportioned evil not to one person, but to society. There is no single perspective. A truly postmodern approach. You try to understand the villain. That ancient question asked since the earliest times confronts you: What is the source of evil? This question does not leave you throughout the novel.

An unexpected ending and that ancient question nail you to your spot after finishing the novel. We need such courageous authors and novels to unravel the knots of society. And we always will. I offer my gratitude to Feyza Altun for bringing such a novel to our literature.

Ahmet Uygur

Inspired by true events.

If you see an eight-year-old child reading a book for 10 hours straight without looking up, don't think about how much they love reading, think that they definitely have a problem.

Life is harder for some than it is for others

"Who are "you"?" said the Caterpillar.
Alice replied, rather shyly,
"I—I hardly know, sir, just at present—
at least I know who I was
when I got up this morning,
but I think
I must have been
changed several times
since then."
Alice's Adventures in Wonderland

END

2019, Kartal

> *"But I don't want to go among mad people," Alice remarked.*
>
> *"Oh, you can't help that," said the Cat: "we're all mad here. I'm mad. You're mad."*

Alice's Adventures in Wonderland

It was a hot Thursday morning, four o'clock.

She was tired from the six-hour fight. They had been fighting almost since she put the child to sleep.

She couldn't believe she had actually called her boyfriend and badmouthed her. Because of this, she had been abandoned once again, which was something she could never endure. She had spent two days in the hospital on an IV drip to be able to pull herself together. Sedative shots had only just managed to quell her crying fits.

For her, separation was the same as dying. She even sometimes thought, "Dying is better than separation. At least you know you're dead". Once, she had even said this to a friend whose spouse had died, risking being perceived as rude:

"Getting used to death is easier than getting used to separation."

Of course, her friend had told her she was talking nonsense, but she was sure of her opinion.

Aside from the immense pain of separation, the feeling of the person closest to you stabbing you in the back was also agonizing. How could he not be careful with a subject she was so sensitive about! The moment she heard about the shit he'd pulled, she had gone crazy. Anyway, her life was spent going crazy over what this woman had done. Every time she saw her, heard her voice, she tensed up, exploding with anger left and right.

For years, she had somehow endured what she had done to her, but now things had gone too far. They had reached the point where the boundaries she constantly loosened no longer stretched. This was the red line. Perhaps she had made the mistake in the beginning by taking him back into her life. When she was away from him, she was relatively more comfortable; she wasn't triggered, she didn't suffer in the shadow of memories.

When her friend told her she should never live with him, she had said, "Frankly, I'm not thrilled either, but I'd prefer him over a nanny." Because she was so stubborn, no one around her could object.

She looked at the knife in her hand with disgust.

"She got what she deserved, I'm finally free", she thought. "It's finally over."

She felt so light... She began to think her soul was free, as if her soul had sprouted wings and flown out of her mouth, spinning around the room, waving to her.

Her adult self had taken revenge for her childhood. While her soul somersaulted in the air, her childhood self watched her from a corner of the room. It was her seven-year-old, always-reading-a-book self facing her. She was watching what was happening, slightly anxious, slightly scared, but greatly relieved.

"You don't need to be afraid anymore," she said, looking at her childhood self in the corner.

"It's over now."

***

She looked at Mert Can sleeping inside. He was sleeping soundly.

My beautiful boy…

She went to the bathroom and washed her hands. It was as if she hadn't just killed someone but had woken up at that hour in the morning because she needed to use the toilet. After washing her hands, she walked towards the kitchen. Her feet weren't touching the ground; it was as if she was floating a centimeter above the floor, gliding through the air. Her pain had lessened. But not all pains had ended yet.

She opened the kitchen cabinet under the sink. Pots, pitchers, anything that didn't fit on the kitchen shelves had been placed in this damp area. Dirty water leaking from the sink pipe had filled one of the pots. She broke out in a sweat dealing with the pots.

"I mean, after all, we are a nation that cooks win-win meals, why make cabinets the size of the pots, we can't even make proper cabinets."

She was surprised she was thinking these things. While a woman lay on the floor at the entrance, covered in blood, she was thinking about pots that didn't fit in cabinets and cabinet sizes. She laughed. She had thought she would be scared, panic, or be sad. But the only thing she could think about was the pots.

She took the rat poison hidden behind the pots.

"Oh, my back hurts from bending over. Whatever, soon this won't matter either, you can keep your shoddy kitchen cabinets."

She took a water glass from the glass-fronted shelf. She turned on the tap and filled it with water. Then for a moment she thought about pouring that water out and filling it with clean water from the water dispenser, then she giggled at the thought.

"I'm going to drink rat poison, but please let the water be clean. What weird things am I thinking tonight…"

To get to the living room from the kitchen, she had to pass through the entrance. She looked at the corpse lying on the floor with indifferent eyes. She jumped over it and passed into the living room. She took the medicine bag from the display cabinet where the plates were. She poured all the medicines from the bag onto the couch.

All sorts of antidepressants, sedatives, expired antibiotics…

"Damn, we've taken every medicine on the market. Fuck your medicines, none of them are worth a damn. Clearly, I spent years making you money trying to get treatment… To hell with you, you little tiny bastards! Now your time to be useful has come. Come on then, I'm going to drink all of you at once. Now do me a favor and do something good for once and kill me."

After taking all the pills, she poured the poison from the bag, whose edge she had torn, into the remaining water. She shook the glass until the powder dissolved in the water. Then she downed the contents of the glass in one go. She leaned back. From where she was leaning, she could see both the entrance and her son's room. First she looked at the corpse at the entrance, then at her son.

"You will be much better off without me. Believe me, I will only hurt you. My world, my soul, and my self are shattered."

"You will be much better off without me. Because I sometimes forget you exist, and that causes me great pain. If this continues, when you grow up, you will be a poor person tired of my crises, my mood swings, your mind divided only into black and white."

"You will be someone scattered like me, never able to pull yourself together, trying to find your existence only in the love of others, you will feel sorry for yourself."

"I never knew what I wanted for you, but I know very well what I didn't want. I hope you can forgive me. I love you."

She was turning everything that had happened over in her head. Actually, she had always imagined such an end for herself. Although she would never have wished for this to happen while Mert Can was around, everything had unfolded this way tonight. Thank God she had messaged her ex-husband.

"He's sleeping now, he'll see my message in the morning and come here to get Mert Can. Anyway, the house key is with the cleaner who comes to both our houses."

She definitely hadn't planned tonight this way. At most, she would have kicked her out of the house, watched with great pleasure as she was disgraced on the street, but that look of strange pleasure in her eyes and her saying "This is what you deserved" had been the final straw. Seriously, how could she have tormented her like this her whole life? And most importantly, why?

From where she was, her eyes caught the book in the niche she had designed and had made. "It's good to be an architect", she thought, "otherwise I'd have paid the workmen a fortune for this niche". The book, yes, which book was it that caught my eye just now? I have so many books, which one was it that I looked at just now? Wow, I really read all these books. Because I relied on books all my life. I always read, I sought peace and happiness in them. Or I escaped the void inside me, I don't know. That book there...

She had seen the book she looked at just a moment ago again.

"I read this one countless times. As I read what was described, I said yes, it should be like this, but I think there's a huge difference between reading and practicing. I only read."

Even though she wanted to get up and get the book, her teeth began to ache, her hands began to go numb. She couldn't quite tell how much time had passed since she took the pills and the poison, her eyes fixed on the book, she tried to remember paragraphs from it.

Then she remembered that part she had underlined with a few different colored pens:

"Everything in your life repeats. The same events happen the same way over and over again because you don't want to change them.

You complain again, you blame the world again, and you believe again that someone from outside has hurt you or brought disaster upon you. A person stuck in this cycle of time cannot have a real future; they only have a past that they live over and over again."

"Yes, I believe exactly that," she said in a faint voice.

"I believe that, you bastards, because that's exactly what happened! People brought disaster upon me. Actually, this book's know-it-all, prescriptive tone pisses me off. As if changing the things that happened was that easy! I spent my life trying to change these things, sometimes trying to forget, sometimes trying to confront. None of it worked. But it turned out beautifully. Seriously, isn't it a bit cruel to say that people who suffer don't want to be free from their suffering? Maybe they want to but don't know how to do it? Saying "Change this" is easy, but no one explains how it will happen. Everyone says "Don't be sad" but no one says, "You have a right to be sad; be sad, I'm here with you." These people know everything! I wasn't asked at birth if I wanted to live, nor was I asked whose child I wanted to be. When I was just a little kid, they didn't ask me about anything they did to me, and because of that, I have no control over anything in my life. How funny is it that I don't even have control over what I feel. At least I should be able to decide how I die. The book says death is suicide, what kind of saying is that, I never understood, what does 'death is suicide' mean? If you die even if you don't choose death, does that also count as suicide, or is it a metaphor? And isn't attacking death like this very meaningless? After all, while death is the only phenomenon in this world that can stand firm against everything and sustain its existence... I think death should sue the person who wrote this. It is too proud to accept such an insult. Besides, death is a liberation, it's beautiful ...that was good, I wish I had written it down somewhere. The death of some people is a liberation both for themselves and for those around them. Moreover, let some people commit suicide, it's called natural selection. I wish some people would eliminate themselves like this. But not the ones who are hurt, let the ones who hurt others commit suicide. Let them hug the ones who are hurt. Let them love them. I'm starting to talk nonsense again. How do my thoughts suddenly get so mixed up? Once, during a meeting, a song by Muazzez Ersoy came to mind. The song said, "I left lovingly! I endured the pain for love! If we become happy! Let's make up again." Wasn't that so absurd? When people break up, if they are happy about breaking up, why would they make up! Who writes a song like that? Anyway, I was always very afraid of this. What if we are happy about the separation? It's certain that I won't be, of course. While thinking about this song, I had said "Absurd" to the client waiting for my comment in the meeting. Ugh, how my boss had looked at me with disgust… The cold wind blowing in the room would literally chill you. Oh, the things I'm thinking, these thoughts always make me abnormal. If I could think just a little normally, I'm sure I would be normal too. I always used to say, cut my head off from my shoulders. They didn't cut it. If such an option existed, I would definitely have it cut off. What would happen, it's like getting a haircut after all. Though it's not my fault, it's always because of the *School of Gods*."

Her eyes still on the book, she continued thinking.

"How many Gods are there? And aren't they Gods, why are they going to school? Or are the Gods giving lessons to their weak subjects? The Gods only know how to teach lessons and punish, they don't know anything else. If Gods really existed, would there be pain on earth? I think I'm going to die from a stroke rather than poison. Oh girl, you've already been struck, look you can't even die and you're still thinking nonsense. Forget these things now, just let it go for once. If this head works like this, even poison won't have an effect. Ok. I'm quiet. Am I quiet? Was I even talking? I'm talking, see. As always, I'm talking to myself. Also, why this obsession with sending everyone to school? Just leave the kids alone, brother, these things happen because you mess with kids. My stomach hurts. It used to hurt like this at school too, it happens to me when I get scared. Are you scared? Well done, finally feeling the right thing in the right place, it's late but better late than never. Be afraid. I'm with you, be afraid. You can be afraid. Everything is over now. You can be afraid."

Her eyes had started to roll back. She could no longer see the book, she was slowly losing consciousness. Her body began to

19

tremble, to shake violently.

She died within about twenty minutes.

RUNAWAY

Fatoş, 1948, Şişli

> *"She curtseyed again,*
> *not knowing whether she was speaking*
> *to a mouse or not; this time she heard a little squeaky voice,"*

Alice's Adventures in Wonderland

Fatoş was lucky for a girl of that time because her father sent her to school. She was just eight years old, a bit of a mischievous child. Her mother never hesitated to express, within Fatoş's earshot, that this girl should find a husband instead of going to school, that they were wasting their money and time in vain. But according to her father, Fatoş would go to school and become a teacher.

Fatoş, who had an average level of intelligence, like every child, preferred running around and having fun with her friends, playing hide and seek, and racing bottle caps rather than studying. She didn't seem capable of showing the success her mother expected from her and was criticized by her mother at every opportunity. Her brother was more practically intelligent and more successful at school than she was according to her mother.

Of course, this was according to her mother because, according to Fatoş, her brother was a little idiot.

Actually, this situation was a big disadvantage for her. Because no matter what she did, her mother's devotion to her brother, who was three years older, always left her in the shadow. By being born a girl, she had lost altitude in her mother's eyes. Unaware that she could only please her with superior success, Fatoş played hide and seek with her

21

friends after school every day, didn't notice how it got dark, came home late, and became the target of her mother's wrath.

When she came home late, her mother would give her a good scolding, and not stopping there, she would definitely pinch her flesh at times when her father wouldn't see. Those little pinches hurt Fatoş more than solid slaps. In those moments, a scream rising from Fatoş's lungs got stuck in her throat, her heart ached because she hated being pinched like that. Just as a person feels discomfort when someone they don't like brings their face uninvitedly close to theirs, Fatoş felt exactly the same discomfort, feeling as if her private space had been violated.

She found this woman, who was supposed to be her mother, somewhat merciless and harsh. While every mistake of her brother's was forgiven, his smallest success was rewarded, her own successes were seen as something that should have happened anyway, and her mistakes were never left unpunished.

Once, when she had a high fever, despite her begging her mother, she was sent to school because guests were coming over, cleaning needed to be done, and she shouldn't be underfoot. That day, she got a bad grade in dictation. Of course, her mother never missed the opportunity to punish her for this failure, immediately bought her brother a rooster-shaped candy, and told Fatoş that she didn't deserve candy because she got a bad grade.

Even though her father favored her, her mother's word ruled at home. They lived in teams of two people each: father-daughter, mother-son. If someone needed to be blamed, they would immediately gang up and start fighting.

***

The school they went to was a neighborhood school close to their home. Every day she would leave home with her brother, meet him at the exit after school, and return home together. Her feelings towards her brother were not unrequited; her brother didn't like her much either.

Her brother was a spoiled boy who thought the world revolved around him thanks to his mother's attention. Therefore, from the moment they left home and walked to school until they left school and came home, they would bicker over at least ten different topics; her brother would pull her hair, and Fatoş would spit on him or kick him.

Her mother, who witnessed her spitting on her brother a few times, would sternly explain that it was very bad for young ladies to behave like that, that everyone would greatly disapprove of her, and that by doing so, she was acting like loose girls. Although she would occasionally slap her bottom a couple of times, Fatoş never deprived herself of the pleasure of spitting on her brother.

Their mother would prepare their lunches in a tiffin carrier every day and always put flavored candy in their bags. In those years when the discovery that sugar triggered cancer hadn't been made yet, quite a few people believed, on the contrary, that it sharpened the mind.

The children would also every day, thinking about the candy they would eat at the end of lunchtime, devour what was in their tiffin carriers, then down the candies with great pleasure. Although Fatoş had seen her brother dump the food from his tiffin carrier into the construction site next to the school a few times at dismissal, and discovered that her brother ate the candies before finishing his meals and complained to her mother, her mother hadn't even considered scolding her favorite child.

At that time, "If I did that, she'd kill me", she thought, feeling resentful towards her mother once again.

One Tuesday of that spring, when lunchtime came, her brother came to her class; even with his jug-handle ears and his senseless existence inside his black pinafore, he could irritate Fatoş. The child asked Fatoş, who was staring at him intently:

"Fatoş, what flavor was your candy?"

Fatoş looked at her brother's face sourly and answered:

"None of your business!"

"Come on, tell me, look, mom accidentally put two in for me, let's swap if you want."

Fatoş, eyeing her brother suspiciously, turned to her bag and looked inside the buttoned compartment. Her mother had put an orange candy today. But she liked banana or cocoa candy more.

She had taken the candy in her palm and turned to her brother when the child, with great cheekiness, snatched the candy from Fatoş's palm and started running.

Fatoş was red with anger. "See", she thought, "I knew I shouldn't have trusted him".

As the child left the classroom, he turned his head and stuck his tongue out at Fatoş with a spoiled grin that extended behind his ears.

"This child is an idiot. His body couldn't spare much time for the brain while those ears were forming", she thought. She was so angry that she muttered, "I know what I'll do to you".

When all lessons were over and it was time to go home, her brother couldn't manage to pack his bag because he was chatting with his friends, he would drag his feet and come to the door lazily. Fatoş, taking advantage of his sluggishness, packed her bag and stormed out of the classroom.

She ran into the adjacent construction site. Bricks stacked on top of each other were covered with a blue tarpaulin. She went behind the bricks and sat under the tarpaulin so passersby wouldn't see her.

Now, when her brother came to the exit gate and couldn't see her there, he would search for her frantically. Since he knew he would get scolded by his mother and father if he went home without her, he could never go home without her. "Oooh", she thought to herself, "now you take your punishment, see. Seek me, find me."

***

The construction workers were mixing cement, carrying things, joking with each other. Even though she couldn't see them, she listened carefully, wondering if anyone had seen her. Even though her legs started to tingle from sitting in a crouched position for two periods, she thought it would be a good lesson for her brother and mother. Let's see what her mother would do in her absence. "Oh, I don't even care", she thought, "let them worry a little".

Just as she stretched her numb legs outside the tarpaulin to stretch them, she saw a pair of feet approaching her. These were definitely not her brother's feet. "Darn, the workers will find me now, then they'll definitely send me home", she was thinking when a 15-year-old young boy opened the tarpaulin.

Fatoş brought her right hand to her lips and made a "shush" sign. She always saw this sign on the nurse photo hanging in the school infirmary. She liked imitating that photo.

A smile settled on the boy's face, which was looking in surprise. Without saying a word, he winked and closed the tarpaulin back. Fatoş saw the boy walking away and entering the construction site.

It was getting darker, and Fatoş's eyelids were getting heavy. With the darkening sky, she began to get scared; she should go home before it got even later. Her mother and brother must have learned their lesson. Also, she couldn't upset her father more while teaching them a lesson. Meanwhile, the construction workers were leaving the area, some going upstairs to their apartments, whose windows were covered with oilcloth, to slurp the tea they had brewed with a half-full picnic gas cylinder.

As Fatoş was getting ready to get up to leave, the tarpaulin opened again. She saw the boy she had seen earlier facing her:

"Come, I'll show you something."

Fatoş shrugged her shoulders, got up from where she was sitting, and followed the boy. The boy had gone inside the construction site. The interior of the half-completed building, which was still just brick, was pitch black. Fatoş asked fearfully, "Where are we going?"

"Come, don't be afraid," the boy said, grinning again.

He lit the stairs leading down with a lighter he took out of his pocket. The light was pale and weak. Only one step was visible where the boy held out his lighter, making it impossible to understand what was below. Fatoş followed him without hesitation.

Down below, to the right of the stairs, piled in a corner, were crates, thinner cans, oilcloths. There was nothing but broken bricks on the ground, dust piles covering everywhere, and walls that hadn't even been plastered yet.

The boy turned one of the crates over onto its feet and sat on it. "Come next to me," he said. His voice sounded more like an order than a request.

Fatoş, feeling like a robot, numb, obeyed the command. Standing in front of the boy in her slightly oversized black pinafore, white collar, and short lace socks, she was still wondering what he was going to show her, thinking, "what could he possibly show me here?"

The boy's devilish hand reaching out to her and the fabric of his worn-out black pinafore from washing were in a strange harmony. One had only been worn for two years, the other was only fifteen years old, yet they seemed as if they had been tortured by others for years, abused for years. This hand, depicting the transformation of the oppressed into the oppressor, was a bad picture reflecting a person inflicting the disgrace they lived through on someone else. Those who experienced evils could only overcome their traumas in two ways; either by doing the same or the opposite. So, the cruelty repeating the evils Fatoş did not yet know had materialized in the vile hand of a boy and confronted her.

The hand wandering over her body on top of the pinafore had taken Fatoş's breath away from fear. She couldn't move, she wanted to scream but couldn't open her mouth as if someone had pressed a button and muted her. The boy's hand went down from the pinafore to the girl's legs.

It was as if he had done this before, had severed the lives of other children –right there, in that dark, dirty construction corner– with a sharp knife, cutting them in half.

The boy's hand pulled down Fatoş's underwear. Fatoş would forget this moment countless times in the rest of her life and relive it countless times again. She didn't know whether forgetting was better or remembering this and fighting with this memory. The boy forcing her to turn her back and sit on that hard thing, and when she refused, pressing down on her shoulders and mistreating her until tears came to her eyes from pain, and while she cried, he just said "shhh" with a strange grunt, had broken her heart. Moreover, whatever he was doing or why, as he moved back and forth, it hurt even more. She never felt any pain in the rest of her life as deeply as this pain. She couldn't decide whether this pain was her heart's pain or her body's.

Finally, the boy lifted her up by her armpits. Fatoş pulled up her underwear and started running without looking at what was running down her leg.

She ran non-stop. She was running with her mouth agape, crying. She was out of breath but wouldn't even stop to catch her breath. It was as if a huge darkness was coming from behind to swallow her, and she was struggling not to be caught. She ran until the air she took in burned her lungs. When she reached the door of the house, she had lost consciousness enough to forget how she got home.

When she got home, she was leaning forward, hands on her knees, trying to regulate her breathing. It was as if her ribs were broken and piercing her lungs. At that moment, she saw the watery blood flowing down her legs to her lace socks. "He cut me. It hurt so much", she thought, "I've been cut". Some part must have been cut!

27

With the sleeve of her pinafore, she frantically wiped the inside of her legs, crying, she rang the doorbell. At that moment, she even loved her mother very much, she wanted to hug her and cry. She would tell what happened, say that brother had cut her. Then her father would know what to do.

She would never want to upset her mother again; she must have been very worried, very upset.

***

"Where have you been!"

A solid slap exploded on her face. Her mother's eyes were shining with fury. Fatoş's lips were trembling, she was afraid to open her mouth.

"I said where have you been!"

The woman slapped her again. Fatoş raised her head and looked inside. Her father was sitting in the armchair, looking elsewhere. Her brother was watching the slaps with a grin. She started crying quietly.

"Look at that state, you're like a corpse! Walk, get lost to the bathroom."

As Fatoş walked slowly towards the bathroom, she could hear her mother's fading voice:

"I'm telling you, this one needs to be married off. What does she need school for, let this one grow up a bit more, look what troubles she's going to cause us."

Fatoş had abandoned the idea of telling her mother, father, or anyone else what had happened to her the moment the slap exploded on her face.

Because she "herself" had "caused" what happened to her by hiding under that tarpaulin. If her mother found out, then she could

28

hit her even more.

Also, it appeared that no one had missed her in her absence. While the reaction she thought they would give upon seeing her was happiness, she was faced with a dark anger. "So my existence only angers them", she thought.

Years later, when she thought about it, she realized that she cried that day for the moment she understood that they were not happy to see her.

RAID

Bedri, 1973, Üsküdar

> *"Let the jury consider their verdict," the King said.*
> *"No, no!" said the Queen. "Sentence first—verdict afterwards."*
> *"Stuff and nonsense!" said Alice loudly. "The idea of having the sentence first!"*
> *"Hold your tongue!" said the Queen, turning purple.*
> *"I won't!" said Alice.*

Alice's Adventures in Wonderland

His chin was bent towards his neck, as if it was constantly growing. An unbearable pain had shot into his teeth. His head felt like it was about to explode. When he opened his eyes, he saw the owner of the hand pressing down on his mouth with all its force. Even though he tried to sit up in panic, the man was leaning on him with all his might; getting up was impossible.

He tried to turn his head to look at the woman and the child but couldn't manage that either. As he tried to move, he realized his hands and feet were tied too. The sky still hadn't begun to lighten.

"Who are these men, why did they tie me up!"

The man pressing on his mouth forced a piece of cloth, whose light color he could barely make out, through his teeth. He tied the cloth so tightly that Bedri thought the place where his lips ended would tear.

Then he held him by the nape and sat him upright on the bed. Then he saw the woman and the child; they had crouched down against the wall opposite the bed, huddled together. Both of their mouths were tied. A person each was holding them beside the child

31

and the woman, although in any case, neither of them dared to move even if no one was holding them.

On that cold December night, even though the woman and child were shivering, the reason was not the freezing air but the terror of what was happening. While the fire from the stove visible from the room's door hit the floor, it was as if an invisible wall had been drawn between; the heat didn't pass to that side at all.

Without saying anything, they started beating the man in front of the woman and child. The man who had tied his mouth had laid him on the floor, was kicking his chest, his stomach, occasionally bending down and punching his face.

Bedri couldn't tell how long the beating lasted, but he felt himself beginning to lose consciousness amidst his groans. The last time he had received such a beating from his father in the village was because of his hair; he had been eager to grow his hair out, his father warned him every day to get his hair cut but he didn't make a sound. That day, as he was going to the coffeehouse, he had called out:

"Bedri, get your hair cut today."

Bedri hadn't paid attention, thinking he would just grumble and then be quiet, but that night while he was sleeping, his father had woken him up with a beating, saying "You son of a donkey, you son of a dog!" and had beaten him until his mouth and nose were smashed.

Moreover, afterwards, with the blunt scissors he got hold of, he had practically plucked his hair out, and Bedri had had to get a crew cut for the plucked patches on his head to fix themselves.

All these passed through his mind in a short moment, his eyes were closing.

When he woke up, he was still lying on the floor. The child, however, continued to sit hunched in the same corner, looking at him with fear-filled eyes. The skin on his face was taut as if a box of glue had been poured on it; "blood", he thought, "who knows how much blood had flowed and dried on his face".

Every millimeter of his body ached, he couldn't move his arm from the pain. Fatoş, while crying hysterically, was dipping the undershirt in her hand into warm water she had poured into a bowl and cleaning the blood from the man's face. "My brother and my husband," she said between sobs.

"Of course", Bedri thought to himself, "how could he not have thought of it". He had received a beating similar to the one he got over his hair, this time for a forbidden woman. According to him, women always brought trouble to his head, but he had a weakness for women. Wherever and however, regardless of the conditions, he could seduce a woman. "But women have a weakness for me too", he thought, with unnecessary pride.

But how had Fatoş's brother and husband found them? He never thought they could find their place, but he inwardly knew that one day this encounter would happen. "Then the police route is closed, you can't go to the police", he thought to himself. In this case, he either had to do the same to them or continue to run away. However, doing the same could prolong this situation, feed the hostility even more. "Let these pains pass first, then I'll look for a solution."

Fatoş cleaned the blood from the man's face with great care. No one was paying attention to the child trembling with fear in the corner. Neither Bedri nor the woman was speaking. Amidst Bedri's groans, Fatoş carried him to the bed; exhausted, he slept for two days without opening his eyes.

***

Two days later, Bedri woke up feeling a bit better. He called Fatoş to his side and began to speak:

"Fatoş, they might come again. Now moving you to another house isn't easy; so let me disappear for a while, if they come again they won't find me, maybe they'll leave us alone."

33

Fatoş didn't like this situation at all. Bedri, whose eye was constantly on the outside, who sometimes spent nights on the streets —or in some woman's bosom— who knows what trouble he would stir up...

"What will we do alone?"

"Nothing will happen, I'll leave you enough money."

Even though Fatoş didn't like the situation, she could not think of any other solution.

"Okay, but don't be gone too long, you know, the girl gets very fussy without you."

Bedri, looking at the ceiling with empty eyes, slowly nodded his head up and down.

***

Three days later, Bedri prepared a small suitcase and hurried to the door to leave. His eye caught the girl watching him by the door. "Come on, we screwed up, but I don't know why we did this", he thought.

"My beautiful girl, come here."

The girl came to her father's side, crying.

"Daddy, please don't go."

"My little lamb, I have to go now, otherwise the bad men will come again. I'm going now but I promise, I will definitely come back, and I'll bring you a doll when I come."

The child started crying even more now. The possibility of the bad men coming again had almost driven the child crazy with fear. She clung to her father's leg, begging him not to go, not to leave them alone.

Fatoş was watching this scene from a distance. Allowing the child to dangle from her father's pants for a while longer, hoping he might take pity on the child and not go.

As Bedri tried to extricate himself, realizing nothing would stop him from leaving, she furiously pulled the child by the shoulder, separating her from Bedri's pants.

"Alright, safe travels, goodbye," said Fatoş.

"Goodbye," Bedri replied.

REUNION

Aynur, 1975, Üsküdar

"Curiouser and curiouser!" cried Alice (she was so much surprised, that for the moment she quite forgot how to speak good English).

Alice's Adventures in Wonderland

She was five years old. She had been lying on a chair at the police station for exactly two days. The police approached her with great affection, constantly gave her candies, and tried to make her laugh. However, she never laughed, looked ahead with a tearful face without raising her head, muttering to herself.

It had taken the people at the station two days to find the child's father because no identification for the child had been found at home, and it had been extremely difficult to get her father's name and surname from her. The child wouldn't open her mouth.

For two days before coming to the station, she had sat by her mother's corpse in her pajamas, trying for a long time to wake her up. Although she inwardly knew her mother wouldn't wake up because after so much blood had flowed, something very bad must have happened to her. "Blood, blood, blood is flowing", she was delirious. Moreover, her mother wasn't breathing and was getting colder and colder. "Mom is getting cold, mom got cold, mom became cold". Even though she couldn't make sense of what these meant, she inwardly knew that something was extremely wrong.

Her mother's face was as usual. She looked a bit angry, and a bit as if she loved her. Since her eyes were open, she had bent over her countless times, trying to understand if she could see her.

According to her, since her eyes were open, her mother must be seeing her. But she couldn't understand why she wasn't reacting even though she could see. Sometimes her mother did that. She would look at her but say nothing, not react. Her mother had gotten angry with her father and bitten her arms. So, a couple of times, she brought her arms to her mother's mouth. Parting her cold lips, she touched her flesh to her teeth. Nothing was happening. Anyway, her mother didn't look angry like she did those times when she bit her. Then she touched her arms to her lips. Because she would kiss those places where she left marks after biting. "If she's not biting, maybe she wants to kiss", she thought. Her mother didn't do that either.

"Mom is sulking with me, that's it. She's not talking to me because I let her bleed so much", she thought. She brought cheap, single-ply toilet paper from inside. She started sticking toilet paper to the bleeding places. This way, she would stop the bleeding and show her mother that she was taking care of her.

Her mother did the same when she bled somewhere. She spent the first day sticking all the toilet paper onto her mother's body. Then her stomach hurt. Her height didn't reach the counter, the shelves, or anywhere else. She pulled the curtain under the counter and started eating bread. She brought a piece of bread to her mother too. After holding the bread to her mother's mouth, thinking she couldn't bite such big pieces, she stuffed smaller pieces into her mouth. Even though she tried to open her jaw, she could only throw a few crumbs between her teeth, which seemed locked.

She pushed, poked, cried over her mother lying under a mountain of toilet paper, and finally became convinced that she would get no response from her mother. She was now sure that her mother would not talk to her, maybe even to anyone.

"I think they will put mom under the ground. As mom said, they bury those who don't breathe."

She spent the first night with her head on her mother's chest, which remained under the pile of white paper. She just fell asleep silently, with her innocent thoughts in her little mind that couldn't make sense of events.

When she woke up in the morning, she climbed on a chair and poured the water she took into her hand onto her mother's face. Then she slapped her mother's cheeks a bit. Her mother still didn't react.

"Mom is gone now."

At the end of the second day, when she was sure she was getting no response from her mother and that she was gone, she started crying and screaming, the neighbors crowded the door, trying to get her to open the door by giving instructions. However, even if the child could turn the key in the lock, she couldn't remove the key from the lock, and she couldn't reach the chain behind the door.

The door was opened by the fire department. Some of the neighbors started screaming at the top of their lungs when they saw the corpse lying in the entrance, some started crying. One of the firefighters immediately informed the police and urged the neighbors to feed the child's stomach.

The child, scared by the screamers, started crying out even louder. No one could calm the child down.

***

Two days after that, her father showed up; he was pale. He looked at the child, whose flesh had clung to her bones from fear and worry, with pity.

The child, however, had fixed her beautiful, almond-shaped eyes on her father. "Dad is here. My beautiful dad, my dear dad. Thank goodness you came. I love you so much… You won't leave me now, will you? Oh dad, I was so scared! Who were they, dad? What did they do to mom?"

She was looking at her father with the appetite of a street animal whose stomach was stuck to its back from hunger. She wanted him to look at her, to look and never turn his eyes away. She needed those eyes, the trust, the warmth that would flow from those eyes to her. She needed to hear from her father that she wouldn't be abandoned again, that she would always be loved, that she would always be happy.

"Come on, girl, let's go," her father said.

He had whispered at length with the police, made heated hand gestures, and finally his face had fallen a bit. While the child watched him carefully, he turned to the police and said, "Let me handle these matters, I'll come."

***

After leaving the station, they went down to Üsküdar market. Her father was carrying the child in his arms. The child had put her head on her father's shoulder, her arms dangling down. She was so frightened and tense that she relaxed as if she had been given a sedative and fell asleep on her father's shoulder.

First, they entered a store whose owner was her father's friend:

"Welcome, Bedri Bro, is this your little one?"

"Yes, Halim, get her some clothes quickly."

He woke the child and sat her on a chair. Halim, seeing the bloody pajamas, raised his eyebrows in surprise:

"What's going on, Bro, did you have an accident or something?"

"Hush now, just get some clothes for this child."

Halim carefully started taking out clothes suitable for the child's size onto the counter. They took off the pajamas and threw them in the trash. They dressed the child in red-bowed shoes and a yellow dress with white polka dots and left the store. They loaded up on underwear, shorts, sneakers, and a couple of toys from the market and finished their business.

She was so happy to be with her father that it seemed there was nothing left to worry about. From now on, they would have a life together, just the two of them. Now that her mother was gone, her father wouldn't keep abandoning her like this.

"Will you eat, my girl?" her father asked.

"I will," she said timidly.

They sat in a pide restaurant. The child ate and drank whatever was put in front of her without breathing. Her father watched the child in amazement, enjoying feeding her stomach at the same time. After eating, they entered a children's park on the way. The child's eyes lit up when she saw the large, crocodile-shaped slide in the park. She ran up the slide and slid down. Then, without getting tired, she slid down again, and again, and again. As if she wasn't the one who had waited by a corpse covered in blood for two days, she giggled, looked at her father from afar, and waved. While she was recording this moment, which she would remember as one of the most beautiful memories of her life, as the crocodile slide, her father bought buttered corn from a passing vendor. The child continued climbing the slide with corn in one hand.

The man looked at his watch, flicked his cigarette towards the trash container next to the bench.

"Sweetheart, come on, we're going home."

"Home?"

"Which home?"

"Are you taking me back to that house, dad?"

"What other home would we go to besides our house?"

The child's face suddenly changed:

"Which home?"

"Come on, we'll talk on the way."

Her father was holding the girl's hand, walking calmly. While holding his daughter's palm in one hand, he kept tugging at the bags with the other:

"Don't worry, you won't be going to that house, this is a house where you'll have lots of fun."

"I knew it. I knew you wouldn't leave me again, I knew we were going to a nice house."

Her heart was filled with peace, a smile spread across her face. She gripped her father's large hands tightly with her small hands.

CHILD HOME ALONE

Serkan, 1990, Üsküdar

"if you don't know what to uglify is, you are a simpleton."

Alice's Adventures in Wonderland

"I'm asking you, why did you leave the child?"

"I didn't leave her, ask your mother, ask her to explain!"

"What am I supposed to ask my mother? The child is bruised from crying, my mother had to call a locksmith to open the door, have you gone mad!"

"How can they lie like that, how! And you only believe your mother! If you believe her, then why are you asking me, get away from me!"

Aynur pushed Serkan and headed towards the door of the house in a fury. She slammed the door shut with a great noise and left the house. Füsun and Serkan looked at each other in silence.

"I'm going to go crazy, Füsun, this woman is going to drive me insane."

"Calm down, my dear Serkan, calm down, let's find out the truth of this matter."

At that moment, Füsun's Terrier breed dog started barking. The small dog was barking at the door with great self-confidence, as if it were the largest living being in the room and could rule over everything.

Just then, the doorbell rang. It was Serkan's mother.

"Was it you who barked?" Füsun asked Serkan's mother.

Serkan and his mother looked at Füsun with blank expressions.

"Oh, I meant to say, did I bark at you, for heaven's sake, is there any mind left… Sorry, please excuse me," Füsun corrected herself.

The tension of the event passed as these words made everyone laugh.

***

When Füsun came out of the kitchen with a tray of tea glasses, Serkan had his elbows on his knees, his head in his hands. "My God, what sin did I commit, and if I did, was it this big?" he was sighing inwardly.

He was 22, his wife was 20. Their daughter had just turned two. That day, his mother, who lived upstairs, had called him at work and told him to come home urgently. Because around noon, his mother had heard the child crying out, had gone downstairs but no one had opened the door. Finally, the mother-in-law, thinking something had happened to her daughter-in-law and her granddaughter was trapped inside, had called a locksmith and had the door opened. However, the granddaughter was home alone.

Serkan had come home and waited for his wife for hours, red with anger, and to stay calm, he had called his wife's closest friend, Füsun, over. His wife, who came home around six in the evening, stubbornly denied that she had left the child home alone. Serkan couldn't understand what good it did for Aynur to claim that something so many people had seen with their own eyes hadn't happened, or what possessed her to do such a thing.

"No, Füsun, if she gave a reasonable answer, I would pull myself together and act accordingly. She just says, 'I didn't leave the child home alone.'"

"Look, Serkan, she's always been like this, but no one bothered. Let's take her to a doctor."

"Let's take her. Let's take her, but she might make that doctor sick too. Let's hope we don't have to take the doctor to a doctor then!"

Aynur was always tense and irritable. She was unhappy. She was the embodiment of unhappiness in material form. Neither kind words, nor peace, nor opportunities made her happy. In the face of lack of opportunities, she never knew how to be content with what she had. Generally, her motivation was money. Serkan had learned this and since that moment had been calming her down by giving her money. During this process, he worked more, found more peace.

There wasn't a healthy dialogue between husband and wife anyway because Aynur seemed not to hear him. She didn't even seem to be aware of Serkan's existence. She would look at his suggestions, everything he tried to explain with kindness and goodness, with disgust, as if looking at a dead rat. When he was sure she didn't understand or wasn't listening to what he said, he would end up having to beat her. Beating her really relaxed him. "So my father must have felt this relaxation when he beat me." When beating didn't work either, he would leave the house, leaving Aynur and the child alone. Then he would be left alone with the guilt of beating her, and when he thought that this wasn't a way, that the wounds opened in his soul by the beatings he received from his father hadn't even healed to this day, he would run to Aynur to apologize. Serkan would promise himself after every fight that he wouldn't raise his hand again, but he could never keep his promise.

He began to keep this promise he made to himself repeatedly when he saw the bruises on his daughter's body. When he realized that violence didn't come from heaven, that it only made Aynur worse and that she was also applying this violence to their daughter, he deeply regretted what he had done, but it was too late. Their daughter had become a constantly crying, fussy, and unhappy child. One day, he sat Aynur down and gave a long speech of regret, asking her to promise him that she would never beat the child again.

Aynur had stroked this compassionate hand extended to her, held it, and valued it. It was truly one of the rare moments of agreement between them. But because Aynur couldn't evaluate events as thoroughly as Serkan, she didn't give up beating the child for a long time. She would take out her anger on the child, whether she was angry at her mother-in-law, Serkan, or anything else. The child sometimes wouldn't react to objects thrown at her, and if the beating didn't hurt too much, she would continue playing indifferently.

As Serkan couldn't stand this situation, he began to distance himself from them. He didn't know how to deal with Aynur. Even though he wanted to protect the child, every closeness he showed her was met with hostility by Aynur, who would then verbally abuse the child. He found escape in running away, in distancing himself.

***

Serkan actually hadn't wanted to get married. If it were up to him, marriage wasn't even an option. But as a last resort to silence his mother and father, he had chosen this woman. At the beginning of their relationship, she was an extremely dazzling, fun, and attentive woman. Though the beginning of the relationship he referred to was two months before their marriage. "You got married in two months, you idiot. Son, people get engaged for this reason, to see each other's flaws. They test each other, weigh each other, decide whether to get married or not. Why on earth did you get married within two months! And even if you did, why did you have a child right away?" he constantly thought, berating himself.

Actually, it was all his own fault. He had thought, "I'll marry a quiet woman, establish an order, silence everyone, and after establishing my dominance, I'll continue with my life."

He had friends who did this. Their wives would wait at home with dinner ready, raise their children without being too demanding, and his friends would party wherever the night found them. He thought he could live that too. Besides, this was more masculine-powerful, more attractive. It was a fantastic opportunity to show his mother, father, and everyone around him that he could be like everyone else, that he wasn't problematic, and that he was, of course, adaptable. But the plan hadn't worked out.

He was now sure he didn't know what a strong man was like. He was helpless, hopeless, and anxious. It was only certain that he was trained in beating, humiliating, and running away. Every time he felt cornered, even if he didn't hit Aynur anymore, he would humiliate her, trigger her traumas, and when he couldn't cope, he would leave the house and not return for days.

This marriage game, which he thought would establish his own state and seemed harmless at first, had slowly turned into a nightmare. Now he couldn't take a step towards divorce. Divorce meant failure. What would everyone say? Society saw people who couldn't sustain a marriage as incompetent or flawed. Besides, he no longer had the energy to deal with his mother and father.

Fortunately, he loved his little daughter. She had a tiny nose and huge eyes like his. He felt like taking her and squeezing her inside him. This was the only genuine feeling he felt from the heart in this fraud. Aynur's hostile attitude towards him because he loved their daughter tied his hands and feet, and he tried to stay as far away from the girl as possible.

***

A few hours later, Aynur came home. As if nothing had happened, she threw her arms around Füsun's neck and asked how she was. Her mother-in-law was looking at her with weary eyes. She gave a small kiss on Serkan's cheek and kissed her mother-in-law's hand.

"What are we drinking, Ece?"

After getting herself a tea, she started gossiping about the downstairs neighbor she had met. Everyone watched her without a sound, even laughing at some of the things she said, partly out of anger, partly so as not to spoil her cheerfulness.

When everyone left, Serkan turned to Aynur and spoke:

"If you do it again, I'll break my promise, I'll break your legs, understand!"

The woman smiled silently and nodded her head up and down. Her eyes were shining as if she had been complimented, not threatened.

ACCUSATION

Figen, 1994, Kadıköy

> *"Off with her head!" the Queen shouted at the top of her voice.*

> *Alice's Adventures in Wonderland*

"You, may God curse you, may God curse you a thousand times!"

She threw the remote control in her hand at the child's head who was studying on the couch. Aynur was on the verge of going mad with rage. Her eyes had grown large, her face had turned red. At that moment, she had no connection left with the world. She had detached from reality; it was as if she had been locked in a dark room with steel walls. She was crashing into the walls at the cost of tearing her arms apart, running from one wall to another without thinking what would happen. These crashes would bruise her flesh, and she would regret it later, but she couldn't control herself, she only relieved her soul with fury.

The remote hit the child right on the head. It had hit so hard that the batteries flew into the air. Figen jumped into the air at once, both from fear and pain. It was the umpteenth time of verbal and physical violence from out of nowhere. A period of regret and fawning would follow. All this made her feel worthless and, most importantly, unworthy of love. Although she had learned to endure the violence and its extent, she hadn't learned not to be afraid. Because you never knew when or where the anger outbursts would come from, and this situation caught her unprepared. Of course, most of the time, these baseless explosions also took away her hope that everything could be beautiful. As days passed, she became more pessimistic, she became uneasy when everything was going well.

She turned to her mother and spoke calmly:

"What happened?"

"Your father isn't coming home because of you. You went to your father and said, 'Mom beats me,' look, the man isn't coming home. I'm sick of you! Everything would have been easier if you hadn't been born. Your father loved me so much then! You, you are a curse, a curse!"

Tears welled up in the child's eyes. A terrible feeling of guilt and helplessness paralyzed her. She knew that if she answered, she would face a bigger outburst of anger, and if she didn't answer, she would be accused of not taking it seriously. At times like these, she just wanted to disappear. Sitting upright on the couch, she was looking blankly at the palms she had placed on her knees. She felt so helpless and worthless during these anger fits that she always wished she had been born as someone else's child. She could have been the child of Emine's mother at school, for example, or Betül's. Because their mothers neither threw remotes at their heads nor said bad things like "I wish you hadn't been born". Even though she was only six years old, for six years she had only heard words from her mother about how her birth was a disaster, and she couldn't feel any bond with this disconnected, indifferent, and mostly mentally distant woman. This situation was also painful for her. The more she couldn't love her mother, the guiltier she felt, and while other children loved their mothers so much, she attributed her inability to love her mother to her own abnormality. Wasn't her mother always confirming this anyway? When she shared her thoughts with her, her mother would definitely say she was a strange child.

"What kind of a child are you, who do you take after, I wonder?"

Whereas she just loved to daydream. She would dream, hold onto those dreams, and write scenarios about them. Because she read a lot, these scenarios were always rich. But her mother didn't think so, she emphasized that she was different.

While all these were passing through her mind, she hadn't realized she was crying hysterically. When her mother started walking towards her upon hearing the sobbing sound, she shielded her head with her hands and begged, "Please don't hit me, mom!"

Her mother slowly sat next to her on the couch and tried to lower her hands:

"Look here..."

Her mother's voice was soft and calm. The child lowered her hands with curiosity, suspicion, and distrust. The storm had subsided. Now her mother would offer her something, try to act as if nothing had just happened.

Without saying anything, she turned her head towards her mother, trying to calm herself down by counting the patterns on the carpet.

"Look at me, my dear girl."

The child raised her eyes with difficulty. She had to be cautious against the possibility of her mother having another anger outburst at any moment; she could suddenly shout, beat her, accuse her, or have a crisis and throw herself on the ground. Her displays of affection were usually passed off with one or two head pats without exaggeration. Providing the basic food and hygiene needs for her survival was the entire finesse of childcare for her mother.

At times like these, she really wanted to be with her father. Her father was always calmer and more smiling than her mother. Also, she felt that he inwardly hated her mother too, and thinking she had an important common ground with him on this issue, she felt close to him. Although her father didn't pay much attention to her either, this calm man sometimes taking her on his back and pretending to be a dog entertained her very much. Yes, she definitely loved her father more than her mother. Her mother must have noticed this too, because she did everything to keep them apart. When they read something together or played with toys with her father, her mother would cause problems over a message she found on her father's phone, pounding her hands and feet on the ground, stamping on the carpets, or locking herself in a room and threatening to commit suicide, thus drawing all her father's attention to herself.

At such times, Figen was upset not so much that her mother might die, but that her father would pay even less attention to her. She was also very angry with her mother. Her mother would immediately take away the little happiness she had achieved in her life, cutting her short-lived happiness right in the middle like a knife stab. She really didn't understand why her mother behaved like this, but she swore that if she ever had a child, she would definitely not be like her mother.

Especially this suicide business interested her a lot. Her mother would try to commit suicide when she didn't get her way. As far as she understood, this could be done by taking pills. In fact, recently at school, she had explained to her friends what suicide meant and was very surprised that her peers didn't know it. Because she herself had witnessed her mother attempting suicide a few times and had saved her twice. Even if she didn't love her mother, she certainly couldn't let her die, but she couldn't help thinking "I wish she could succeed" sometimes.

All these complex emotions proved to her that she was an abnormal and bad child.

"Your father upsets me so much, girl. Look, he didn't come again today. What time is it anyway… Never mind, I'm not angry with you, would I ever be angry with you? Shall I heat some milk for you? Come on, let me heat some milk. And may God curse that father of yours, may he die wherever he is, in whose bosom he is."

The girl's eyes widened like saucers with fear. "May my father not die, God, please don't let him die." She wasn't sure whether being left alone with this woman scared her more or never being able to see her father again, but she was pleased that the woman had suddenly become affectionate towards her. Trying to be worthy of this show of love, she said, "Okay, mommy."

She was afraid of angering her mother again by saying she needed to finish her homework, so she left her books and notebooks right there and tiptoed to the kitchen to taste the bestowed mercy.

Did her mother love her or hate her? While the place where the remote had hit was still throbbing, she wondered curiously if her father really wasn't coming because of her. "Sometimes thinking about these things makes me very sad. I wish there was someone I could tell these to." But if she told someone and that person went and told her mother, the outcome would not be good at all. She was feeling down.

Every day, every moment, she constantly felt like crying. While her friends ran and played cheerfully, she would daydream thoughtfully and read lots of books. Seeing that there were girls like her in some fairy tales relaxed her a bit. Like Cinderella in that fairy tale, who was despised by her stepsisters. I wonder if a fairy would come to her one day too?

Maybe with a magic wand, she could turn her mother into a loving person who didn't beat her. Or she could make herself a good enough child that her mother wouldn't have to beat her. Then her father wouldn't neglect to come home, and they could live a happy life together.

However, there was one thing her mother was proud of her for and she was sure of it: her success at school. So Figen never risked this, she constantly studied. She studied so much that her parents couldn't keep up with providing her books. Sometimes she would compete with herself, set a time limit, and count how many words she read by that time. She had already learned to read before starting school. Although her teacher wanted to start her directly in the second grade, her mother hadn't allowed it. "Why didn't she allow it, it would have been so cool, I could have said to everyone, I'm so smart, see, I skipped first grade directly, what's up, smarty?" she thought while drinking her milk...

I LOVE YOU BUT

Nihat, 2019, Tarabya

"I wish I hadn't cried so much!" said Alice, as she swam about, trying to find her way out. "I shall be punished for it now, I suppose, by being drowned in my own tears!"

Alice's Adventures in Wonderland

"I love you very much, you are the love of my life, but we can't make this relationship work. It's not working, don't you see? The smallest problem turns into a big crisis, we're not good for each other."

The woman was looking at Nihat in panic. Nihat continued:

"Look, I'm irritable too, I'm tense. I'm not good for you. In those moments, whatever you're going through, something comes out of you. I can't calm you down, then I lose my temper too, you see, we always end up at the same point."

A strange smile spread across the woman's face.

"My dear," she said, "you misunderstood me. You're right, I exaggerated the situation a bit. I promise it won't happen again. You know my mother…" she paused. "Anyway, never mind my mother now. Believe me, I understand my mistake."

"No, Figen, no, don't start with that mode," said Nihat.

"It's always the same things. For three years, I've lost myself because of you, my mental health is no longer normal. One moment you're fine, the next moment I see that look in your eyes without understanding what happened. Such a dark look that… I'm afraid of you now."

"You're afraid of me?" the woman asked.

This time her voice was trembling with anger. Her understanding and sorry state was slowly giving way to anger.

"Anyone hearing would think you're a saint."

"Okay, I'm not, you're right. I made mistakes in this relationship too, but now I see that we're not suitable for each other. I have the right to break up too, don't I?"

"You do, of course," she said in a dry voice, "you do, but breaking up because you see an imaginary dark look in my eyes is an obvious lie. Does anyone break up with the woman they love over something like that!"

"It's not imaginary, it is!" shouted Nihat. Uncomfortable with his own voice, he looked around to see if anyone had heard.

"I see that darkness, it goes so deep, I'm afraid to learn where its bottom is."

"Don't talk stupidly, Nihat, you might as well start a witch hunt like in the Middle Ages. What is this!"

Nihat wanted to interrupt, but Figen didn't let him:

"Of course, I'm your Satan, aren't I! Don't you dare call me again! I didn't even hear something this humiliating from my ex-husband I divorced. You will regret this very much, Nihat, don't forget. You're leaving me for who knows who now, don't worry, the truth will come out, you'll come crawling back!"

Figen had said these in an increasingly rising tone. After finishing her words, she angrily threw her things into her bag and got up from the table. She was shaking with anger. Figen, while loving Nihat so much, couldn't make sense of his constant desire to leave her; separation caused her great pain. Figen never wanted to separate from Nihat. According to her, if Nihat were a bit more understanding when problems arose, it would actually solve all problems. But he was stubborn. Nihat deserved to be miserable, he would be miserable...

***

Nihat looked after Figen with relief. He was glad she didn't start crying and begging because then this chapter never ended, the conversation turned into hours of whining and efforts to persuade.

Even though Nihat never wanted to make Figen experience these things, he never knew how to deal with Figen. He didn't know what she wanted, what he was doing wrong. He had done everything he could, offered her everything within his capacity and means. However, Figen was always lacking, always unhappy, always demanding. This situation also tormented him. He wouldn't fall in love like this again, but another truth was that he could never be with Figen.

"A perfect woman; intelligent, fun, beautiful; she has a lot of things many women don't have, and I… God damn it, I've never loved anyone like this in my life. How can she not see this… Nothing I do is enough, nothing I do can please her. Every time the same fight, the same disgrace. Her eyes… While looking so beautiful, a hellish flame suddenly starts burning inside her. Either she's a real idiot or she's sick. The other day, for example, when we went to dinner with İsmet and his wife, she was so cute, so affectionate… But when we got home in the evening, she started a fight because she said I looked at the woman at the next table."

I'm not even aware there was a woman at the next table. I don't understand how she thinks these things, how her brain works. She's very attentive to her son, but sometimes she acts as if he doesn't exist, how can a mother forget her child's existence? I'm not used to these things. And then she says 'for who knows who'. The day I met her, I closed the page on other women. I wanted my life to end with her. In my eyes, there is no woman on earth who could make me forget her. How could she be so fixated on other women, how can she not see my love for her… What kind of pain is this, God, in her heart, where is that successful, intellectual architect woman I knew, where is this

57

insecure, sick woman; I never thought disappointment could mess a person up so much…

He shook off his thoughts and picked up his phone. He called İsmet; after ringing a few times, the phone was answered:

"Hello, İsmet."

After summarizing the situation for a while, they arranged to meet in Karaköy in two hours.

He got up slowly from where he was sitting and went to the cashier. He wiped the tears in his eyes with the back of his hand so no one would see.

***

İsmet and Nihat sat down at a raki table. Nihat was so quiet and distracted that İsmet didn't speak at all, calmly waiting for his friend to get to the point.

Just then, the light on Nihat's phone lit up. It was Figen calling.

Nihat took a deep breath, took the phone, and got up from the table, looking at İsmet with apologetic eyes.

"Yes?"

"Nihat."

"Yes."

"Nihat, I love you so much, please let's not break up."

"Hey, weren't you the one who talked and talked and left me in that dump of a place?"

"Yes, but you were talking nonsense, I couldn't stand it, sorry."

"Enough already, I'm not your toy, Figen, always the same old story, enough."

"Nihat, my dear, please calm down, look, I've reflected on and thought about the issue deeply; I can see you're right, I'm so sorry. You know I love you very much."

"It's not a problem about love, Figen. I love you too, but it's not working, it won't work. Nothing will ever come of us, Figen!"

"How can it not work! Why shouldn't it? Do you have to be so negative all the time?"

"Look, we've talked about these things countless times. A million times even... I'm tired now. I'm out, please, let me be, we'll talk later, okay?"

"Look, I'll tell you something, one minute."

"Go on, then."

"I'm sorry, I love you."

"Okay, we'll talk later."

"So you forgive me?"

Nihat was getting really angry:

"Look, I'm asking you not to push me, please, just give me some space, hang up the phone."

"I will, but look what I want to say…"

"Saaay!" he said, drawing out the word.

"You're right."

"Look! Are you making fun of me, shut up now, just shut up, hang up."

Nihat was now red with anger.

"But Nihat, the way you behave…"

"Beep beep beep…"

Nihat had angrily hung up the phone. "No, this woman won't change, this woman never understands a word", he said to himself.

Was it that hard to understand? How hard could it be to give a person time, to give them space?

After going to the toilet and washing his face, he returned to the table. İsmet could see how tense Nihat was but didn't dare to ask. Nihat started without needing to be asked:

"Bro, it's always the same thing! The woman doesn't understand. What part of 'give me some space' don't people understand, İsmet? She doesn't understand, she doesn't give space, she doesn't break up, my soul is suffocating, İsmet, do you understand?"

İsmet intervened in a tone meant to calm his friend:

"Tell me this story from the beginning."

Just then, Nihat's phone started ringing again.

Nihat rolled his eyes; it was Figen calling. He didn't answer the phone.

"We broke up, İsmet, this woman doesn't change. No matter how much I explain, it's as if they've taken the brain out of her head, she doesn't understand me."

Just then, the phone started ringing again.

"Look, she'll call like a pervert all night long," he said, shaking the phone towards İsmet's face.

This time the call was short. But now messages were coming one after another.

"I love you so much Nihat. Please let's not break up. We are meant for each other."

"Nihat, can you pick up? I have one last thing to say."

"Nihat please look, one last time."

"I love you, always love me. I can't bear being without you."

"Where are you that you're not answering, I'm going crazy."

Nihat wasn't reading the messages anymore. He almost knew all the incoming messages by heart. Soon, Figen would convince herself that Nihat was with another woman and start attacking him, then apologize again and send love messages.

He dropped the phone, put his elbows on the table, and buried his face in his hands.

"It's so hard, İsmet, doing this is very hard for me too."

"Brother, I understand," said İsmet. "You also abandon the girl every time, this girl clearly overreacts when you leave her. Look, either don't leave the girl, or if you leave her, don't go back, bro, anyone would lose their adjustment."

"You're right, I know. I love her so much that after a while I forget every bad thing that happened and again fall under her spell, but thanks to Figen, it doesn't last more than a month that we get along well. But, İsmet, I can't tolerate these strange states, I want to run away and distance myself. If only she would let me be, give me some space, maybe I would miss her and call her the next day."

This time, İsmet's phone started ringing. İsmet, turning his phone screen towards Nihat, asked, "It's her calling, should I answer?"

"Don't answer, leave it, she'll talk for an hour now," he said.

Then Nihat's phone started ringing again. Then again, and again, and again... That night, Nihat's phone rang until its battery died.

CEMETERY

Fatoş, 1974, Üsküdar

"She was always fond of pretending to be two people. 'But it's no use now,' thought poor Alice, 'to pretend to be two people! Why, there's hardly enough of me left to make one respectable person!"

Alice's Adventures in Wonderland

It had been almost a year since Bedri left home. The money had run out. Fatoş was going to houses to clean, trying to feed her child. It was impossible to ask her family for help; wherever she called for Bedri, they would say, "He just left, sister-in-law." Of course, Fatoş knew Bedri was telling them to say this. She was aware that he was more afraid of getting beaten up than he was of God, that he was crushed under this responsibility, and of course, that he was chasing after other women, but she couldn't quell her anger.

"But he was married, Fatoş, we told you," said the woman, putting her coffee on the table.

"I know, I know, okay, shut up!" said Fatoş.

"And you are married too," the woman continued in a careless tone.

"Yes, but I left that house, I bore him a child, and I stated many times that I belonged to him."

"You really left your two children behind and gave birth to this one, and you're telling it as if you've done something great."

"What should I do, sister, he didn't want my children!"

"Good for you, you left your children because some man didn't want them, then you go crazy when he leaves you too. Very logical!"

While the two women sipped their coffee, the four-year-old child was playing quietly with her toys on the carpet.

"Look, girl," said her friend, "divorce your husband, and let him divorce his wife, then you get married. You threw away the other two, at least take care of this one."

She pointed to the child sitting on the floor.

It was easy to say. She knew, of course, about divorcing and marrying him, but she couldn't even approach her husband to say this. He would kill her. Hadn't they come and beaten Bedri? That night, her husband had whispered in her ear, "Your turn will come too." How could she divorce this man? And even if she divorced, would Bedri get divorced? The man had left the house once, and that was it, impressive. He wasn't even worried about what they would eat or drink. She felt hopeless that he wouldn't divorce to marry her.

***

Fatoş called Bedri's workplace tirelessly every day. Each time, his coworkers would answer the phone, never put Bedri on, and hang up with excuses like "he just stepped out, he'll be back soon". But today, Fatoş had no intention of hanging up without speaking to Bedri. Someone else answered the phone again:

"Hello."

"Hello, is that you, Nazmi? Is Bedri there?"

After a short silence, "Bedri didn't come to work today, sister-in-law," said Nazmi.

"I know he's there, tell him I know how to come there myself, but I can't bear to pay for three buses. I'm taking his child to Karacaahmet now. He has one hour to come and get her, whatever he does. I'm leaving."

She hung up on him without waiting for a response. She started crying so hard from anger that her saliva was flowing, and she was shaking with uninterrupted moans.

She changed the child's clothes, left their house in Çiçekci, and started walking towards the Karacaahmet Cemetery. Fatoş kept tugging at Aynur, who was trying to keep up with her pace. The child followed her mother, stumbling along without a peep.

When they reached the cemetery gate, she nodded to the guard at the gate and went inside. She took the headscarf from her bag and wrapped it around her head haphazardly. As she walked, she tried to see if the guard was watching her. The guard had already forgotten them, swinging his prayer beads in his hand.

They went down the left fork right in front of the mosque. Walking among the graves, they looked right and left as if searching for a grave to water and pray at.

"Mom, what is this place?" asked Aynur.

"A cemetery," replied Fatoş.

"What's a cemetery?" she asked innocently.

"A cemetery is where the dead lie."

"Mom, what is dead?"

"If you stop breathing, you die, and they put you under the ground. Now hush!"

The child looked at the lands surrounded by white marble in fear.

"So there were people who no longer breathed between these marbles."

"Why do they put people in the ground? When does a person stop breathing? And what if they want to breathe again later? Maybe they are sitting in a room under the ground, that's why they can breathe later, I wonder how they get out? Will they put us in this ground too? If my mom and dad are in this ground, I'll be alone and scared, I definitely don't want to go in. Even if I don't breathe, I want to stay in our house."

The child's heart was beating so fast that if one listened carefully, her heartbeat could be heard in the abandoned silence of the cemetery.

They stopped at a distance where the gate was still visible. Fatoş turned to Aynur:

"Now you will wait here. Do you see the gate? Don't take your eyes off it. Your father will come, he will take you. I have some business, I will come to get you from your father after I'm done, okay? Call out to your father when you see him so he knows you're here."

Aynur started to cry. Tears began to stream down her eyes like thread, her mouth wide open. Her mouth was so open that when Fatoş slapped it, a dull sound was heard. Aynur's eyes grew even wider, but her mouth closed.

"You will stay here if I say you will stay here. Don't talk to anyone," she said.

As soon as she finished speaking, she turned her back and quickly walked away.

Aynur was on the verge of going crazy with fear. If she were an adult, she could have said she lost her mind from fear. But since she didn't yet know how to name her emotions, she just cried.

"I don't understand at all why my mother left me here. When will dad come, can the people under the ground see me now, when will they come out, what if they try to force me in there too? I won't go in, I'll resist. I'll hit them, I'll beat them like those men beat my dad. I can breathe, no, I won't go in there."

For hours, she stood still, afraid to even move, as if paralyzed, trying to breathe.

She didn't know how long it had been since her mother left; a child that age naturally couldn't tell. Although there were no words to describe her fear, Aynur was having a panic attack. It was starting to get dark.

It seemed to her as if the people under the ground were trying to get up, the ground was moving. With the street lights turning on, she mistook the shadows of trees hitting the white marbles for ghosts trying to pull her down.

Aynur had been in the cemetery for a full five hours. The effort to remain breathless that had started five hours ago was still continuing; she was struggling to breathe, her chest tight. She was exhausted from this effort, her face almost turning purple.

There was no one coming or going. She was afraid to move from the spot where her mother had left her, watching hopelessly for her father, whom she expected to enter through the cemetery gate.

That day, her soul was split in two. It was torn, wasted, like a piece of paper ripped irregularly from top to bottom. This white paper, on which beautiful writings, instructive formulas, perhaps other languages could have been written, was torn and thrown away while still blank. The fact that from the outside a physical wholeness was visible caused the truth that the child's interior was shattered to be overlooked; especially if this was a quiet, calm child. Without knowing that Aynur would never recover for a lifetime, Fatoş, out of her anger, her fury at Bedri, had used her daughter as bait, but Bedri didn't even care.

Later, Aynur would say to Bedri, who would devote himself to religion and constantly go on Hajj, impliedly, "Go, go, you'll clean your sins by performing tawaf."

While Aynur was still standing her ground during who-knows-which hour of this long wait, her mother appeared at the gate. Fatoş started running towards her daughter with a horrified expression on her face. The guard threw an expressionless glance at the woman who had come to the cemetery for the second time that day.

When the child saw her mother, she was so relieved that she fainted on the spot. Fatoş picked up the fainting child and started walking.

"Oh, my child, have you been here for hours… Oh, my little lamb… See, this is what your father is like. See how much he loves you. Wake up, hey, I'll tell you these things too. He didn't even come to get you, see! As if we left not you but a trash bag there; he doesn't deign to! Oh, my beautiful child, you're cold as ice too. Can a person be so cruel, so heartless? I'll wash you nicely now and put you to sleep, tomorrow nothing will remain. Besides, look, you're so small that you won't even remember today when you grow up. Sleep now, my sweet daughter, sleep."

REUNION

Aynur, 1975, The Village

"I could tell you my adventures—beginning from this morning," said Alice a little timidly. ...it's no use going back to yesterday, because I was a different person then."

Alice's Adventures in Wonderland

They boarded a bus from Harem with her father. On a journey whose duration she couldn't guess, peaceful but sad, she had lain on her father's lap and fallen asleep.

They arrived at a place that looked nothing like anywhere she had seen before. From there, with bags in their hands, they walked to a house with plastered exterior walls. The children playing in front of the door screamed "Daddy!" and ran towards the man when they saw Bedri.

After kissing each of them one by one, Bedri looked around, and just then a woman with a flower-patterned flannel skirt pulled up above her waist, her flesh plump, appeared at the door. The woman first scrutinized Bedri, then Aynur. She slowly approached them.

After the children kissed their father and chatted with him for a bit, all their attention focused on Aynur. The woman, clasping her hands on her chest, said, "Welcome."

The children surrounded the woman and began examining the two of them with questioning eyes. Bedri was the only one who found this strange encounter normal.

Aynur looked at the children who called her father 'daddy' with hatred and jealousy. Bedri turned to Aynur and said, "These are your siblings, and this is your new mother."

"My new mother?" Aynur thought to herself. "Does one just suddenly get a new mother like that? Are mothers separated into old and new? And these children? They're looking at me badly, who exactly is a sibling, am I supposed to love them?"

Aynur looked at the woman her father called "mother" for a long time but with empty eyes. The woman said in a hissing voice, "Her face is filthy with dirt, move aside, let me wash her."

The woman wanted to scream instead of washing the child. Her husband, the father of her four children, who had abducted her from the field and sinned with her when she was only fourteen, who had cheated on her countless times and brought these women home and made her serve them, had now brought his child from another woman home and wanted her to raise him? How long would this child stay here?

It was beyond her control; she was looking at the child with hatred. Who did she look like, her mother? Was this the child of the woman he stayed with when he didn't come home? She wondered where her mother had gone that she had come here. Since Bedri's marriage certificate was with her, this child was illegitimate. So had he set up a life with that woman? Was that life better than this one? Was Bedri supporting another household while they were living hand to mouth? Question marks swirled in her head, a huge lump in her throat, moving back and forth, trying to choke her.

Bedri made a "come here" gesture with his head to the woman. They moved to a corner, leaving the children alone there, and began whispering.

Meanwhile, the children were still looking at each other. No one made a sound. The four children surrounded Aynur like a gang with a maximum height limit of one meter.

The tallest one, Bayram, said, "You are not our sibling."

Aynur pursed her lips. She didn't want to cry but was very scared. She was just experiencing her emotions, which she couldn't articulate or even make sense of, and this made her very uneasy. A deep feeling of loneliness enveloped her. When she lowered her head and looked at her hands, she saw there was still blood under her nails. She brought her hand to her mouth and sucked her finger. A dirty iron taste came to her mouth, mixed only with the taste of the corn she had eaten in the park. "I wish it had my mother's taste", she thought. "It has no taste but it has a color, I guess I need to wash my hands", she thought to herself.

***

"They killed her," said Bedri.

"For what reason?" asked the woman.

"I don't know, I'll find out. I took her from the police station," he said, pointing at Aynur with his head. "Now they've made me a suspect, I have to go back. You wash her, clean her, polish her, let her get used to here."

The woman nodded her head, helpless but expressionless. She turned towards the children. She called out to Aynur, her voice had softened:

"Come, my girl, come, let's clean you, rest a bit too. Are you hungry?"

Even though she was so angry at Bedri that she wanted to grab him by the shoulders and shake him until his brains came out of his ears, she couldn't be angry at the girl. This frightened, startled, filthy child knew nothing about anything.

"Oh, by the way, Aynur has no birth certificate, we'll register you as her mother in the population registry. We'll handle it at the district office when I return," Bedri called out from a distance.

The woman nodded her head in astonishment. "This is a test", she thought to herself. "You are great, my Lord, you must have a

71

reason", and she put the sullen child into the washbasin in the bathroom. She was so distracted and hurt that she didn't even hear Aynur's screams as she passed out, refusing to undress.

GUEST

Figen, 1994, Üsküdar

"No, no!" said the Queen. "Sentence first—verdict afterwards."

Alice's Adventures in Wonderland

After drinking her milk and going to bed, Figen fell into a deep sleep that night. Towards morning, in her dream, she saw a black horse waiting for her under a rainbow and heard it calling to her from afar. She was surprised the horse could talk; moreover, its voice was familiar:

"Aren't you going to come anymore?"

Figen was looking at the horse in surprise and delight, undecided about whether to go or not. But then she noticed the horse was starting to get angry. The horse was now stamping its hooves on the ground where it stood, swishing its tail with fury. Its voice was like fire poured into notes:

"I said come, damn it, come!"

She opened her eyes in fear. Her mother was shouting at her father on the phone. Those years, mobile phones that cost five times the minimum wage were not yet common. There were home phones with cords dangling curled up from the side table, but only a few people had those brick-like mobile phones with antennas up to a meter long. This also gave Figen's father the opportunity to disappear; her mother could only reach him at certain places.

Aynur hung up the phone and stormed into Figen's room angrily.

"You're not up yet! Look what time it is! Let me tell you, you'll never amount to anything, I swear. You'll wander around aimless like your father, or we'll marry you off, and you'll eat husband-beatings all your life. Get up!"

Figen got up and dressed silently. While getting dressed, she was thinking about her father. Actually, she loved her father. Because he didn't torment her, he always spoke laughing, and he kissed her. But since her father stayed as far away from home as possible, he couldn't spend time with Figen. Even though Figen loved her father, she was angry with him for leaving her alone with this woman all the time. Even though she was angry with him, she got even angrier at her mother when she badmouthed her father.

After getting dressed, she took the book "The Crow and the Fox" from her desk and went to her mother.

"Mom, I'll finish this book today, will you buy me a new one?" she dared to ask.

The woman looked at the child sourly and said, "We'll see."

Aynur was setting the breakfast table furiously. "You go down and get some eggs from the grocery store," she said to Figen.

Figen said she would be late for school. In that first year she started school, she was an afternoon session student; she was busy packing her bag and completing a homework assignment she had left unfinished. Besides, she didn't like going to the grocery store at all; she was a somewhat lazy child. But reading and studying were the only things she wasn't lazy about. She read a lot, did her homework without anyone having to tell her.

While her mother was setting the table, she was trying to make a helicopter with a blank squared page she had torn from the middle of her notebook.

She had rolled the body, was trying to glue two paper sticks made into cylinders onto the body with glue.

When Aynur came to the living room to call Figen, she saw the child working on the model and flew into a rage. She furiously snatched the model from her hand and flattened it between her two hands:

"You're going to be late for school but you're playing with paper like a retard, is that it! Go to the grocery store, get eggs."

Figen didn't cry much when her mother beat her, but she couldn't hold back her tears when she destroyed her creations like this. Her mother was taking away from Figen anywhere she tried to escape to. She felt lonely, a great void forming in the middle of her heart. Such a void that every feeling other than pain fell down into that void, unable to hold on.

Figen went to get eggs, crying. When she returned, her mother had calmed down. Smiling, she said to Figen, "Come on, don't be upset, I'm going to your father's workplace towards evening, Nazif will come to look after you, you can play with him."

Boiling water poured over Figen's head. "Nazif shouldn't come."

"Brother Nazif?" she stammered. "Don't let him come, I'll wait for you alone."

"Girl, don't talk nonsense. Besides, he said he'll bring you a hamburger, see, you'll eat it, you'll like it. Wait for me nicely, okay, my girl?"

The child, afraid to show her mother how devastated she was, shouldered her bag and left the house. She walked absently towards the neighborhood school on the corner. She was still in first grade. "Brother Nazif...", she thought. "I hope he doesn't come, I hope he doesn't come, I hope he gets hit by a car, I hope he becomes paralyzed so he can't come. Let me count to fifty now, if I enter the school gate exactly at fifty, let him not come."

She started running...

She entered the school gate exactly at fifty. Her heart filled with happiness.

"He won't come", she thought to herself, "he definitely won't come."

"But if he does…"

If he forced her to swallow those painful white things again, then she would bite him very hard, she thought to herself. Besides, how could this be, she couldn't make sense of it. Her male friends' penises at school weren't like that. She also looked at her father's penis sometimes. When she looked at it over his pants, she couldn't see such hardness.

"Maybe there's something wrong with Brother Nazif", she thought. Anyway, it seemed very meaningless to her that those white painful things came out of a person's body. "There must be something wrong with him" because no other brother forced her to sit on his lap like that. He didn't touch her chest. And he didn't try to lick her lips. Besides, his mouth smelled very bad.

She couldn't ask anyone these things, she tried to find answers by herself. She wished she could tell her mother, but her mother would definitely get very angry with her, so she especially couldn't tell her mother.

Figen decided she was disgusted by Brother Nazif. She went to class.

***

That evening, when Figen came home, she found Nazif at home. Moreover, her mother really wasn't home. She was trembling with fear, afraid to take off her pinafore and get changed. She went into her room and locked the door from behind. No matter how much Nazif begged at the door, she didn't open it. She never wanted to see his face, praying for her mother to return as soon as possible.

After a while, Nazif gave up and started watching television in the living room.

When she heard the door being unlocked with a key a while later, a deep relief enveloped her. Her mother must have come. Still, she didn't open the door lock without being sure. Indeed, her mother had come and was telling Nazif something fervently; it was obvious from her demeanor that she was angry. "Oh well", she thought to herself, "at least she came".

She quietly opened the door lock and immediately returned to her desk. She quickly put her notebooks on her desk and began to wait as if doing homework.

Her mother, as she expected, had opened the door and come to look at her.

"What are you doing?"

"Doing homework, Mom."

"Okay, change your clothes and let's eat."

Even though she was safe from Nazif for now, she hated having to eat while looking at his face. She changed her clothes slowly. She had no intention of sitting down to eat. She was going to say "I'm not hungry" and go to bed. She could even fake being sick. Indeed, her mother didn't insist on her sitting down to eat; she closed her room door and left. But a few hours later, she opened her door again and said, "Figen, I'm going to Füsun Sister's. You stay with Nazif Brother, I'll be right back, and before you sleep, Nazif Brother can read you a book."

"No!" shouted Figen. "No, I'm coming too."

"No, Figen, we have business. You can't come, you will stay home."

Figen started crying. Just then, Nazif appeared behind.

"What's this, you've become a big girl, why are you crying, Figen?" he said smugly.

Figen started crying even more. She ran and hugged her mother's waist:

"Mom, let me come too, besides I like the dog, please!"

"I said no, Figen, besides, you're filthy, go take a bath and clean yourself, then you'll go to sleep."

Aynur forcefully pried the hands hugging her waist and pushed the girl away.

"Mom, then you wait, I'll take a bath like this," the child continued crying.

"Okay, hurry up then," she said.

Figen took a quick bath. While entering her room wrapped in a towel, she ran past the front of the living room so Nazif wouldn't see her. She dressed quickly. She wasn't leaving her room. Nazif and her mother, realizing she was out of the bath, came to her:

"Come on, let me kiss you, I'm leaving now."

Helplessly, the child said, "Okay." Her eyes were bright red from crying.

After Nazif closed the front door, he appeared at her room door.

"Come, Figen, I'll read you a book before you sleep," he said.

He closed the door behind him. Reading a book before bed had never been so vilely realized before.

EID MORNING

Aynur, Figen, Serkan, Bedri, 2006

"It was much pleasanter at home," thought poor Alice, "when one wasn't always growing larger and smaller, and being ordered about by mice and rabbits."

Alice's Adventures in Wonderland

The Ramadan Bayram coincided with October that year. At university, assignments and projects had already started. Figen was meeting up with her friends at every opportunity, studying or preparing her projects. She was a successful and bright student. Education had been her ticket out of the swamp.

That morning, she told her mother and father that she would be having the Bayram breakfast with her friends.

"Alright," said her father, "pick up your phone when we call."

She had left her parents alone for the Bayram breakfast, and without even wondering how they would start fighting the moment they found themselves alone, she had quickly left the house.

At that time, having breakfast and smoking a shisha in Fenerbahçe was a very popular activity among university students. When she arrived at the place, she hugged and kissed all her friends as if they hadn't seen each other just yesterday. Among her friends, she was well-liked, and particularly because of her good grades and her air of a teacher who constantly made them study, many saw her as the gem that would ensure they graduated.

Seeing Figen, her male friends said, "Oooo, the cool girl of our school, our sister, has arrived." "Get out of here," Figen smiled.

They gave their orders. As usual, the mischievous ones of the group, Kerem, Sadık, and Berk, were laughing hysterically. Figen couldn't resist asking:

"What have you lot been up to now?"

"Look," said Kerem, "Sadık the idiot crumpled up a napkin and stuffed it in his mouth, he was choking."

The whole table burst into laughter. Berk, turning to Sadık:

"Mate, why did you put the napkin in your mouth?"

Sadık, who had just been saved from choking, answered:

"I was checking if it would fit."

Figen and the others at the table were in stitches.

Kerem turned to the table, "In two years, they'll be calling this one 'architect' and taking him seriously, but this animal will probably swallow the projects too."

The table was ringing with laughter. Amidst the banter, laughter, and conversations about recent projects, they had their breakfast and exchanged Bayram greetings. Just then, Figen's phone rang. It was her mother.

"Come home quickly."

Hearing her mother's voice, which commanded her without even saying hello, made Figen's skin crawl. She immediately moved away from the table and lowered the volume of the phone pressed to her ear:

"Mum, what's happened?"

"Who is Sezgin?" Aynur snarled.

"Which Sezgin?" Figen frowned.

She had no idea who this Sezgin was.

"Don't lie to me, I said who is Sezgin!"

Aynur was screaming down the phone with great hatred.

"Mum, how should I know, are you mad?! Who is Sezgin, I don't know anyone by that name, first tell me what this is about. I'm with my friends, don't embarrass me."

"Come home quickly, you'll see who Sezgin is!"

She hung up on her mother. She was fed up with her mother. She had a hobby of ruining environments where Figen was happy. It was as if her happiness and peace disturbed her mother. Moreover, she had also ruined her calm and distant relationship with her father. Her father had become quite aggressive and had started to act distantly towards her. Her mother was constantly provoking her father, causing the two of them to argue. Figen was counting the days until she graduated from university and got rid of them.

Lost in thought, as she returned to the table, her father called.

"Come home quickly."

"But I've only just got here. You gave me permission, Dad, why are you calling me now, oh just stop suffocating me."

Serkan, in an authoritarian and hate-filled voice, ordered Figen to come home. Figen, realising she could no longer sit at this breakfast table, that they would never give her any peace, returned to the table unhappily. With great unease, she quickly told a lie to her friends. She had become an expert at lying. To fend off her parents' sudden and inappropriate attempts to cause a scene, she told so many lies to those around her... My grandmother's been taken to hospital, my aunt has taken ill, my blood pressure dropped, I'm dizzy, my stomach hurts, I need to study...

She was constantly trying to suppress a scandal. Her mother and father treated her like a three-year-old nursery child, didn't allow her to do anything, never wanted her to go out after dark, but they themselves went out gallivanting around like teenagers.

Once, although she had barely gotten permission for a school

81

meal, of course her father had called before the meal was even over and told her to come home. Even though Figen said the meal had just started, her parents had taken it to the level of harassment, calling non-stop, saying they were going to sleep, they would lock the door, so she needed to come home immediately.

Figen had returned home very unhappy and, to her great astonishment, found her parents weren't home. That day she had been so angry that she sat down and sobbed with a helplessness mixed with hatred. To be free from her parents' selfishness and the psychological – and sometimes physical – torture they inflicted on her, she would have given her right arm. They wouldn't even leave her in peace in her room, coming in every hour to look at her meaninglessly without saying a thing. At such moments, she felt like an animal on display in a cage, and when she asked what was wrong, she got no answer. "Why are they suffocating me?" she thought. Her father always told her it was because they were trying to protect her. They trusted her but didn't trust the world around her. But Figen secretly wanted to say, "with you around, I don't need the outside world, protect me from yourselves", but she remained silent because she couldn't find the strength to deal with the argument that would ensue if she said it.

She was suffocating, suffocating with these two people called mother and father, she couldn't breathe.

She came to the table and started gathering her things, and this time she told a new lie:

"Right, guys, I could never get enough of you, but I have a date with a handsome bloke, I'm off, love you all."

She brought her hand to her lips and blew a big kiss to the table.

Amid the cries of "Aaaa, no way, don't go," she asked the waiter to call a taxi. She said goodbye to her friends and got in the taxi. She felt as if she were going to her own funeral, not home.

***

When she entered the house, she saw her father fuming. Her mother was sitting on the sofa in the living room, arms crossed over her chest, looking at her slyly. The sight of the two of them like this had really unnerved her. Although she was very used to such moments, these situations tired her out so much now that each time she thought the stress would swallow her whole.

"What's going on?!" she said, her voice cracking.

"I said who is Sezgin, you wretch!" Serkan shouted, advancing towards Figen.

This question was starting to get on her nerves.

"Are you taking the mickey? Who the hell is Sezgin, enough!"

"Tell the truth," her mother snapped.

She scrutinised her mother and father carefully. You could expect anything from these two unpredictable people. Her father's balance and mental health had deteriorated over the years spent with her mother, and the father she had loved so much had turned into her enemy. It seemed to her that he was always looking at her and her developing body with malice. And it was highly likely that these unbalanced people would suddenly say, "We were testing you, just kidding!" She had no idea who this damned Sezgin was and not the slightest clue what was going on.

She took a deep breath for the last time and managed to say calmly, "I don't understand what you're talking about, and I don't know anyone called Sezgin, please can you explain?"

Her mother spoke up:

"We know your cold-blooded lies very well, supposedly you're going to be an architect, love, with that attitude you'll amount to nothing, your mind is always on boys, you'll never amount to anything."

"You're engaged, congratulations, you should have called, we would have come," said her father.

Figen started to laugh. She was roaring with laughter.

"Thanks to you, I'd count it as an experience if I could even breathe the same air as a boy, let alone get engaged", she thought to herself. As she was laughing to herself, a stinging slap landed on the right side of her face.

Figen fell to her knees on the spot. She covered her face with her hands and began to sob hysterically. She was a decent person, she didn't hurt anyone, she was bright, hardworking, she had hopes, expectations, dreams for her life. All her friends loved her. Why didn't her mother and father allow her to be happy, why? Why couldn't she enjoy the moment like her friends, why did she constantly face unease, accusation, and violence… If she had money, she would never stay with these two creatures, but she had neither a place to go nor any money. Her entire childhood had passed with beatings and humiliation, she had only studied to escape, seen a good education as essential for a good future and salary, and had worked hard to achieve it. Every day they hit and humiliated her, she was losing her self-respect, she was dying over and over again every moment, every day, she couldn't fix her damaged sense of worth, a huge void was growing inside her.

"You're sick," she said while crying, "both of you are sick, you're getting more sick every day by looking at each other, you nutters!"

This, instead of calming her parents down, had made them angrier. This time, her father punched her in the stomach. Figen helplessly drew her knees to her stomach and waited for the torture to end.

***

On the second day of Bayram, her mother woke her early:

"Come on, get up, we're going to your grandfather's."

She knew what she was in for if she said she wasn't going now, so she got out of bed reluctantly. Because her grandfather Bedri was a Hajji, she put on something loose and long. Otherwise, he would inevitably complain: cover your waist, cover that, don't show this. Figen found it more logical to take precautions beforehand rather than endure the nagging.

Aynur and Serkan were ready, waiting for Figen by the door. Dragging her feet, she followed them to go and kiss hands at her grandfather's...

The main reason Figen disliked Bayram visits was that her mother always got into a reckoning with the past with all the relatives and inevitably ended up arguing. Her questions and accusations never ended, the ghosts of the past constantly stabbing the living of the present. She particularly couldn't manage to learn about the murder case, whose details weren't told to her and which her mother used as an excuse for her every behaviour, but this time she was determined to find out what had happened from her grandfather.

Living constantly in the midst of tension, Figen didn't want to spend Bayram days like this either, so she always took a book with her, and after kissing the hands of the elders, the eyes of the little ones, and the cheeks of her peers, she would retreat to the quietest room and read.

Because her grandfather lived almost on the outskirts of the city, the journey took a good hour and a half. When they arrived, she remembered unhappily how crowded her grandfather's house was on Bayrams. All her aunts, cousins, and uncles would pile into the house. Naturally, she wasn't sure if she would be able to catch her grandfather alone.

***

Grandfather Bedri had aged considerably. His belly was taut like

85

a balloon filled with water. She never understood how his thin legs carried that belly. With his white lace skullcap on his head, his mesh socks on his feet, and the lumberjack shirt he wore over his tracksuit bottoms that had left marks on the knees, he was like a film character. All her aunts buzzed around their father, not daring to contradict their bedridden mother.

She had been very surprised when she learned that her grandmother wasn't her real grandmother. Although her mother kept her distance from her siblings, she had always spoken of her stepmother with affection. She had favoured her over her own children, taken her everywhere as her first choice, had literally deprived herself to feed and clothe her.

Moreover, this woman had also looked after Figen a great deal. Her hands were calloused from serving, she had done nothing for herself in her later years, and had finally ended up bedridden. This self-sacrificing woman, far from the evil stepmother image in Turkish films, had treated them all as if they were her own child, her own grandchild, even loving them more than the others.

"Why are stepmothers always so bad in those films anyway?" Figen thought to herself. There was a maliciousness even in the intonation of the word 'stepmother'. It was actually a trap set by the mentality that opposed divorce. Sometimes, while a birth mother could treat her child like a devil, a person who hadn't given birth to her but had raised her in her heart could behave like an angel.

Well, her grandmother represented that angel. Figen felt an incredible admiration and love for this woman.

***

After the rush of Bayram greetings in the crowd was over, Grandfather Bedri had withdrawn to his room to pray. Figen had been very surprised when she heard her grandfather's youth stories and couldn't comprehend how that womaniser had become a Hajji. Wanting to atone for his sins, religion for him was not an end but a means, as is the case for everyone. He constantly went on Umrah, investing his money in Hajj tourism while his children struggled in misery. Although her aunts didn't want to say anything, her mother voiced this situation aloud, "However many times you go on Hajj, Dad, those sins won't be cleansed," and things would heat up.

Bedri had been a selfish man all his life. He was harsh, grumpy, and stubborn. After going to Adıyaman to repent, he had started living a conservative life, deciding to return to his lawfully wedded wife and live a settled life. But the traces of the past hadn't been erased for anyone; everyone silently kept reliving and remembering what had happened.

She entered the room where her grandfather was praying and sat on the chair behind the man who was prostrating. The moment his prayer ended, she would ask her grandfather her question without anyone seeing.

She approached him slowly after he said the final greeting, "Grandad," she said. Her grandfather loved Figen very much. He also showed particular care towards Aynur. Whether he felt sorry for the life they had lived or saw this too as a reason for his own sins and sought absolution, Figen never really understood which it was.

"Grandad, I'm going to ask you a question, my grandmother, my real grandmother, my birth one, how did she die?"

Whenever the subject of Fatoş came up, Bedri would get upset, the colour of his face would change. He felt as if he had contributed to a murder, as if they had killed her together.

"Where did that come from now, my little rabbit?"

Her grandfather always called her his little rabbit. When she was little, her grandfather had made a nest out of an old television box, and Figen would eat carrots and cucumbers inside it and hop around, playing at being a rabbit.

"I want to know, Grandad, Mum talks about it every single day, every day."

"Love, it's all in the distant past, I don't even remember."

Although Bedri never wanted to talk about the subject, he was aware that he couldn't escape these curious eyes. But he didn't know what or how to tell.

"How can someone not remember such a thing, please don't disappoint me."

Bedri started to talk. Today, he was skipping the parts that didn't conform to his own values and beliefs, narrating the event as if it had nothing to do with him, sugar-coating it. You'd think he was telling a fairy tale, not a murder.

Apart from this Bayram visit, Figen wasn't allowed out anywhere for ten days. Figen, who was effectively under house arrest for about ten days, begged her parents to let her go to her classes, but she couldn't succeed in any way. As her phone was taken away too, she couldn't speak to anyone. For days she cried helplessly, cried and cried, accumulating hatred inside. Moreover, she had no idea why she was experiencing all this!

When the lockdown ended and everything returned to normal, her mother and father acted as if nothing had happened, as if Figen hadn't faced the risk of having to extend her studies by a term because she couldn't submit her projects due to them.

On the day her punishment ended, her father knocked on her door with all his affection and asked:

"Love, shall we go to the fish restaurant by the sea as a family today?"

"Alright," she said.

She didn't want to go to the fish restaurant, the cinema, or even heaven with them, but she accepted their offers because refusing them always had bad results. Anyway, refusing didn't help; wherever her mother and father went, they dragged her along with them. They wanted to go on holiday and forced Figen to go too. She rebelled against why she couldn't stay at home alone and in peace. Sometimes she wanted to say to her parents, "If the issue is me having sex with someone, I can do that by saying I'm going to school too," but she kept quiet to avoid ruining her academic life.

"How stupid these mothers and fathers are, honestly, if a child sets their mind on something, they'll do it so that no one will know. Instead of trusting her, setting the conditions and rules and letting her go into life, why do they drag their children around with them unhappily like a handbag..." she thought.

Reluctantly, she got up and got dressed, taking a book with her to read. Because she wouldn't be able to tolerate the slightest conversation during the meal.

She put her favourite wavy silver ring on her index finger.

***

At the fish restaurant, her father ordered her favourite fish. Apparently, this meal was a small act of penance. Her face was always sullen. Her family thought she was an ungrateful, aggressive, and problematic child. And then they couldn't understand why this child was like that.

Figen, on the other hand, would usually be amazed at how they could fail to see what was really happening. She was amazed at how they couldn't see that she was unhappy because they threw her around like a stress ball, took all their anger out on her when they fought with each other, and battered her like a punchbag.

Her father's eyes were locked on the ring on her index finger. His face grew increasingly serious.

"Sezgin," said her father.

Figen felt like screaming.

"Again? Is that why you brought me here?" she protested.

"You're wearing Sezgin's ring," said her father through gritted teeth.

Figen looked at her hands in shock. She only had the wavy silver ring on the index finger of her right hand.

"Take it off, give it to me," said her father.

Figen immediately took off the ring and gave it to him.

"Look," said Serkan, "what's written inside?"

Figen frantically snatched the ring from her father's hand.

Inside the ring was written Sezgin! It was as if cement had been poured over Figen's head and had instantly set, leaving her unable to move. She stared at the letters:

S-enselessly

E-xtinguishing

Z-est, zeal

G-ripping me into a whirlpool

I-nhuman offspring Sezgin,

N-ot you, the shameless one

The letters spun before her eyes. Was this Sezgin they were talking about just six stupid letters inside a ring? Was that why she had risked being a term further away from her dreams? Was that why she had been beaten and punished?

"I bought this," she said, stammering with anger, "from the jeweller downstairs."

She pointed towards the rows of bead shops on the seafront.

Serkan looked hesitantly in the direction Figen pointed.

Figen continued:

"This is either the name of the person who made the ring or the brand. But ultimately, I bought it myself and I absolutely do not know anyone called Sezgin."

"Anyway," said her father, "eat your salad, don't spoil our enjoyment."

BETRAYAL

Aynur, Figen, Nihat 2017

> *"'The master was an old Turtle—we used to call him Tortoise—'*
> *'Why did you call him Tortoise, if he wasn't one?' Alice asked.*
> *'We called him Tortoise because he taught us,' said the Mock Turtle angrily: 'really you are very dull!'"*
>
> *Alice's Adventures in Wonderland*

Figen had become a successful, well-known architect in her field. Shortly after her son was born, she got divorced and began experiencing the difficulties of being a working mother. The nannies she found would sometimes not show up for work without notice, she had to go to the construction site with the child, and was subjected to the disapproving looks of the workers. She was also worried about safety at the construction site.

After the terrible problems she had with nannies, for a while she had taken the child to her office too, but both her colleagues' unpleasant attitudes and her partner's words implying this situation was inappropriate left her no choice but to call her mother helplessly.

"What's the matter, you wouldn't call unless you needed something," Aynur answered the phone.

"Mum, please, no snide remarks. I can't find a nanny for Mert Can, and you're struggling too, let me give you the money I'd give to a nanny, come and look after Mert Can. You can't get your maintenance from Dad. We'd both be a bit more comfortable."

Although everyone around Figen warned her to stay away from her mother, she had been forced to rely on her.

Aynur had come running to look after her grandson. The fact that she didn't do even a tenth of what she had put Figen through to Mert Can put Figen's mind at ease. This was because she had mellowed over the years and also because she loved her grandson very much.

But since Aynur had arrived, the tension hadn't ceased; on the contrary, it had escalated. The two women fought constantly, insulting each other. Figen had lost the calmness of her youth. She had turned into someone who behaved exactly like her mother, however she acted. She shouted and screamed, got angry with the child and pushed him around, then regretted it. Moreover, her mind was so confused and busy that she sometimes forgot to pick the child up from nursery, only realising with regret that she had a child when the school called.

She was quite angry with herself for a while for having a child. Although she always said it was impossible to raise a healthy child without being a healthy person herself, she had also fallen into this error. How could she be a mother to a child whose existence she constantly forgot?

She had been with Nihat for the last three years. They had a stormy relationship, on and off. Figen had filled the growing void inside her with Nihat. She was attached to him like a child. She loved him so much that she had built her whole life around Nihat. Her child was practically secondary. She planned her day according to Nihat, slept according to Nihat, woke up according to Nihat.

At the beginning of their relationship, Figen, as in all her relationships, was a lively, cheerful, and understanding woman. Very soon, things began to change, they began to make irreversible mistakes in the relationship, thus opening unhealable wounds. Figen would obsess meaninglessly over Nihat's past relationships, jealously insane over every woman he spoke to, and they would get into endless fights.

At the end of all these fights, Nihat found the solution in leaving Figen, but he couldn't bear it and kept returning to her. The fact that Nihat couldn't break away from Figen made her think she could get away with anything, increasing her outbursts with each passing day.

Despite various madnesses like attacking Nihat kicking and punching in front of everyone at a party because of the delusion that he looked at another woman, keying his car from end to end, trying to set his house on fire, Nihat couldn't give up on Figen.

Nihat also had a side that provoked Figen, but he was a man a woman with a tranquil soul could get along with. Of course, it wouldn't be easy. Nihat was someone with high standards, many expectations, who wanted to receive a lot but give little. He preferred to be loved rather than to love, and that's why Figen's pathological attachment to him seemed attractive to him. Their relationship, pushing and pulling each other, had tired and sickened everyone around them.

Nihat was very tired of Figen's inconsistent attitudes and sought solace in other women to get away from her. While doing this, he was very afraid of Figen and took extreme care not to get caught.

Their last separation had lasted a long time. Both were fed up with each other and had vowed not to reconcile this time. Both Figen and Nihat had started seeing other people. Moreover, this time they weren't even doing it secretly; both gave the impression they were happy in their relationships. However, neither was happy. Nihat saw Figen in his dreams every night, always dreaming that he was hugging her, that they started walking hand in hand. Without exception, he woke up at 6 am from this dream and then couldn't get back to sleep. He would look at the woman next to him, and seeing it wasn't Figen, his heart would ache.

"If only Figen could be calm like that? If only she didn't cause scenes, didn't constantly drag us into scandal... I miss her so much. Her smell, her gaze, her intelligent conversations..."

He remembered a poem by Attilâ İlhan and then recalled those lines:

"Whoever I love, it's you, alas"

"For some reason, one cannot give you up..."

Getting used to life without Figen was very difficult for Nihat. But being with Figen was also very difficult. _I don't know if I am her punishment or if she is my curse, but God didn't make us meet for nothing, He must have a reason_, he thought, trying to distract himself with other things.

Nihat was much better than Figen at occupying his mind. Figen thought obsessively about Nihat, followed his every step, asked about him to anyone who might have news. She treated the people she saw poorly, and because she talked about Nihat for hours, no one wanted to see her a second time. This made Figen feel even more rejected, causing her to become more determined.

After three months, they talked and got back together. They had missed each other terribly. They made love and snuggled for days. Before the same fights emerged in an even more intense form, Nihat had begun to believe that everything could be beautiful.

But nothing turned out as Nihat had imagined. Figen became fixated on the woman Nihat had seen. This time she followed her, questioned what they had experienced, made Nihat's days and nights hell. The most innocent jokes turned into major crises, nights turned into inextricable nightmares. Nihat began to feel overwhelmed again, regretting returning to Figen. Figen never admitted that she had also seen others when they were apart – which was somewhat justified – but acted as if Nihat had cheated on her.

One day, Nihat couldn't take it anymore and said he wanted to break up. Figen responded with a reaction he never expected:

"You're to blame for staying."

Nihat had left the house quietly that day. To clear his head, he met up with İsmet again, told him what had happened and shared his troubles.

Strangely enough, that night Figen hadn't harassed Nihat at all, hadn't sent a single word via message, hadn't called even once. Nihat was both pleased by this situation and a bit uneasy at the possibility that this time Figen might have cut him out of her life. Although he wanted to break up with Figen, he couldn't bear the thought of her being with someone else; this thought drove him mad. Nihat didn't actually want to leave Figen. But being with her was turning into a terrible torment with each passing day. He didn't want to live such a life either.

That night, he drank his rakı calmly. Unaware that in a few hours a phone call would shatter him, he kept drifting off into the distance.

***

Later that night, Nihat's phone rang. It was Figen.

This time, without any reluctance, he answered the phone eagerly.

"Hello."

The voice wasn't Figen's.

The caller was Figen's mother, Aynur.

"Nihat, love, are you free?"

"Yes, go ahead, Aunty Aynur."

"Love, we're at the hospital."

Nihat felt as if boiling water had been poured over his head. Had something happened to Figen?

"Nihat, can you come?"

Nihat said a quick goodbye to İsmet and hit the road. He kept repeating to himself, oh Figen, oh, oh stupid Figen…

In the observation room in A&E, Figen was lying with a tube inserted from her nose to her stomach. The thin plastic tube hanging down her throat was clearly hurting her. When she saw Nihat, she turned her head away.

97

"Figen," said Nihat, holding her hand. Figen wouldn't turn her head, wouldn't look at Nihat's face.

"Figen, my beautiful, look at me…"

Figen, as if she had taken a vow of silence, neither spoke nor looked at Nihat.

"Figen," Nihat said again, "I love you so much, how could you do this to yourself, how could you think of leaving me without you… Don't do this, we'll have better years together. Don't, my beautiful, don't be cross with me, I love you more than anything, believe me…"

Figen, with silent tears streaming from her eyes, squeezed Nihat's hand.

They were sick, but they were also lovers…

THE FUNERAL

Serkan, Aynur, Bedri 2018

"She quite forgot that she was now about a thousand times as large as the Rabbit, and she was as much frightened as if she had been all her life a little girl."

Alice's Adventures in Wonderland

Aynur hadn't been to see her father since the Bayram visit. She had cut ties with all of them, severing the invisible strings that made her act like a puppet of the past. These strings, for her, were her relatives. They all reminded her of her painful childhood and the troubles she had endured.

Her father kept calling her, asking her to come see him. He had even explicitly said a few times that he was very afraid of death and asked for her forgiveness.

These words, more than making Aynur sad, inflamed the fire of revenge inside her, and she chose to punish her father by staying away rather than going and granting forgiveness.

As in everything, she couldn't show balance in this either, leaving Figen's insistence, "Go, see Grandad," unanswered meaninglessly.

"He can't cover up the rubbish he's done so easily now," she had said to Figen one day.

"If we're going there, think about how you're going to cover up the rubbish you've done," Figen had retorted.

This response had caused an argument between them; her mother started telling the same story again, saying Figen didn't know what she had been through, how many days she had stayed alone with her mother's corpse, started talking about her bloody pyjamas, and Figen had shouted at the top of her voice in response, "Enough already, this story makes me sick!" The argument ended when Mert Can started crying, and both women fell silent.

Figen was uncomfortable with her mother's hostile attitude. Her grandfather had aged and was about to die. She thought there was no point in upsetting a dying person. Moreover, her grandfather had always been warm towards her and had always warned her mother for beating her. So, secretly, she even felt grateful to her grandfather.

"You don't understand unless you live it yourself, that's the thing", Figen thought. She didn't consider her grandfather, her deceased grandmother, the grandmother who raised her, her mother's drama, and her mother's endless painful childhood memories as important enough to justify her mother treating her like this. She wasn't exactly a wonderful mother herself, she knew that, but she was proud of herself at least for not beating Mert Can. She didn't humiliate him either...

Using her childhood experiences as an excuse, her mother had tormented her all her life, and everyone around her to whom she complained about her mother had somehow justified Aynur by saying, "But she's your mother, think what she went through in her childhood." Figen had desperately wanted to be understood, had tried to explain that all this was too heavy for a child's body and mind, but no one took her seriously, no one saw the agony she endured.

Because even when she was very small, she was considered wiser than her mother, the expectation that she should behave almost as if she were her mother's mother had deeply wounded her, prevented her from living her childhood, and perhaps she had experienced even more trauma than the trauma her mother lived through.

Her mother had had a difficult life, but that trauma had ended at a certain age in her life. She herself, however, had been a victim of systematic mistreatment spread over years. Her mother had taken out all her ambition and grudge on her throughout her life, had distorted all her perceptions, broken her personality, split her soul in two.

Now, it angered her that her mother acted like an innocent child towards her grandfather. Then, she thought, she herself might also have the right to hate her mother and cut her out of her life in that way. But she was sure that if she did that, she would be condemned by those around her and declared a devil by her mother. This situation drove her even madder.

She was the one who was right, and she suffered every time she looked at this woman. All she wanted was to be understood and to know that her pain was acknowledged. As a child and as a woman, this was all she wanted; to be understood.

***

Bedri had died recently. When her aunts called Figen, she immediately picked up her mother and went to the funeral home. Her mother was fainting and crying, screaming.

Figen was also sad that her grandfather had died, but she didn't have dramatic reactions like her mother, and her mother's reactions made her even angrier. The man had called and asked for her repeatedly; her mother had left these invitations unanswered, hadn't even looked at his face. And now she was crying as if someone who had been by her side every day had died.

She did not, absolutely did not, love her mother.

At the funeral home, they had a hard time pulling Aynur away from her father's body. After everyone had said their farewells to the deceased, they set off to take him to the morgue. The next day, at the noon prayer, Bedri was buried.

Serkan and Aynur met at the funeral for the first time in a long while. Figen had called Serkan and told him her grandfather had died. Being a loyal person, Serkan had come to see off this man who had once been his father-in-law on his final journey.

Serkan and Aynur had divorced long ago. Serkan now seemed calmer, more peaceful, and healthier. After moving away from Aynur, his world had changed, he had found his balance again. Moreover, he had married a year ago and was living his own life.

Seeing Serkan at the funeral, Aynur went mad, attacking him, saying, "You've got a nerve coming, you might as well have brought that whore with you."

Figen was so angry she almost fainted. Because Serkan's wife had nothing to do with her parents' divorce. Her father had met this woman long after they divorced, and her mother knew this very well. Everyone remained indifferent to her uncontrollable, unrestrained, and disrespectful behaviour, and whenever Figen tried to say anything to anyone, she got the response, "You know, her childhood…"

Sometimes she wondered to herself. Can I now use my traumatic past life as an excuse to get away with anything? Can I just do any disgraceful thing out in the open without ever choosing to be better, without trying, without making an effort? Oh, what a wonderful world this is. What a wonderful life!

While thinking these things, it never occurred to her what she had done to Nihat.

Serkan regretted coming, told Figen not to give him such news again, and that he wouldn't come. That was the last time Serkan and Aynur saw each other. It was also the last time Figen saw her father.

At that funeral, Figen understood that her mother had calmed down compared to the past, but the reason wasn't that she had found inner peace; it was because she could no longer batter her and because she was financially dependent on her. If her mother had the opportunity, she would beat her again, torture her again. Her mother hadn't changed; she had only lost her power. No one took her seriously anymore. Two years ago, she had tried to kill herself again, no one had bothered to go to her house, no one had sent an ambulance to her door.

When the ambulance arrived at her door and she made a spectacle of herself to the neighbours, her mother had stopped her suicide attempts.

"Mum won't change, God grant that she dies early," Figen sighed inwardly.

THE TRUTH COMES OUT

Figen, Nihat, Aynur, 2019

"'Collar that Dormouse!' the Queen shrieked out. 'Behead that Dormouse! Turn that Dormouse out of court! Suppress him! Pinch him! Off with his whiskers!'"

Alice's Adventures in Wonderland

Her eyes were fixed on the drip-drip of the IV fluid hanging above. Her older sister-like friend, Füsun, was by her head, stroking her hair.

"My beautiful daughter, is it worth destroying yourself like this, believe me, it's not."

"My heart hurts, Füsun Abla, my heart hurts."

If there was anyone who didn't know what heartache meant, if they could have entered Figen's body at that moment, they would have felt it in all its rawness. How a person's soul can hurt and how this fire doesn't go out found life in Figen's recurring crises.

For a reason she didn't understand, Nihat had left her again. Although Figen should have been used to this pattern by now, on the contrary, she reacted to each separation more strongly than the last. Each time, she greeted the events with as much pain as if it were a new breakup. Füsun Abla had become her confidante; she told her everything that happened and asked for her advice. Füsun Abla gave very good advice, but no one noticed that Figen didn't have the capacity to take this advice and apply it.

Füsun Abla, sitting on the edge of the gurney, spoke:

"My dear, let's go see a psychiatrist from here. You're losing control, don't be upset by what I'm saying, everyone loses control of their life at times, but for Mert Can's sake, you need to quickly regain that control."

"I have no strength left to endure, Füsun Abla, I feel like I'm melting," said Figen.

She really was melting. The emotions she couldn't control, the apocalypse raging inside her, were melting her as if acid had been poured over her.

Moreover, during her last fights with Nihat, she had found herself crying, "Mum, why did you leave me alone?" At that moment, she wasn't angry with Nihat, but with her mother; her reproach, her irritability, her crying, her crises seemed to be just so her mother would see them. When she came to her senses, she didn't even want to remember this situation; she didn't want to need her mother in any way. She often thought about the past, thought about how wounded she was, and how Nihat kept adding new wounds to them, and got angry with him all over again.

What she wasn't aware of, Füsun Abla reminded her that day:

"Love, this isn't about Nihat anymore, you realise that, don't you?"

"How can it not be about Nihat, Füsun Abla, for goodness sake! He's driving me mad!"

Figen tried to sit up from where she lay, but Füsun Abla pressed her hand on her chest, preventing her from getting up.

"No, Figen, you were like this with your ex-husband too, you had similar crises, similar fights, remember."

Figen thought silently. However, she never remembered the time before Nihat; she felt as if she had been the most peaceful woman in the world before him. But no, she thought to herself; she vaguely remembered similar crises. Once, she had become so rigid that her ex-husband had put her in the bathtub with her clothes on and poured warm water over her head, and she only 'opened up' after standing under the shower for ten minutes.

She had experienced similar problems with different people. She experienced these problems especially in love relationships, chasing her own tail like a cat, going round and round without getting anywhere.

Everyone who had tormented Figen since her childhood had withdrawn into their shells and left her life. Her mother, who looked after her child, had also let go of the past and was trying to build a life for herself. Sometimes, when Figen reminded her mother of what she had done to her, she either genuinely didn't remember or didn't want to talk about it. Her communication with her father was practically non-existent. The last time she had seen him was at her grandfather's funeral. And Figen felt that she was the one writhing in the grip of the past right now. The fact that everyone had forgotten everything made her even angrier. They had all poured their wickedness onto her, and now they had withdrawn to their own corners.

Especially her mother, who, as if she hadn't experienced similar things herself, turned her nose up at Figen, and far from supporting her, constantly criticised her about her behaviour, implying that she wasn't a good mother to Mert Can.

"I want to get out of this vicious cycle, Füsun Abla, I really don't want to have these crises anymore," said Figen.

"Okay, sweetheart, the most important thing is that you don't want them anymore. Let me find you a psychiatrist, will you go?"

"Okay, you find one, I'll go."

Figen, with the hope of change in her heart, closed her eyes and fell asleep.

***

After staying in the hospital for two days, Figen felt relieved and calmer. She felt serene and wanted to be determined to change things this time.

Although she didn't yet know what was wrong, so she didn't know what kind of specialist psychiatrist to see, she kept looking up doctors' names on the internet, reading about illnesses and treatment methods.

Meanwhile, Nihat occupied her mind constantly. She hadn't called him yet, but she was forcing herself not to. She had considered calling İsmet a few times but gave up. This time she wanted to do something different from what she always did and surprise Nihat.

But still, she couldn't understand why Nihat had left her this time. Nothing had happened; she hadn't even caused a scene. You could even say things were good between them. Suddenly, Nihat had stopped answering his phone and had left her with a text message.

Whenever she explained the situation to her mother, her face would change and she would drop the subject. "Just leave that man alone, there's no good in him for you, can't you see?" she would say and start talking about other things. Although it seemed suspicious to her that someone like her mother, who loved to milk every piece of gossip to the end, would drop the subject without being curious about any details, she couldn't make sense of it and thought, "she's probably just bored of it".

After all, this was perhaps the fiftieth time Nihat and Figen had broken up. The subject no longer attracted the attention of either her friends or her mother. Everyone listened to the issues rolling their eyes. So Figen didn't dwell too much on her mother's suspicious behaviour.

"If it rains, you'll know it from your mother, Figen, but not that much, leave the woman alone", she thought to herself.

***

Figen and Nihat hadn't spoken at all for fifteen days. The heartache, which should have decreased as days passed, wasn't subsiding; on the contrary, it was increasing. Not knowing where Nihat was, what he was doing, was driving Figen mad. That day, she couldn't take it anymore and called İsmet.

İsmet was always polite to her. He would always answer her calls, if he wasn't free he would call back later, Figen would talk, and he would listen. No matter how badly they had broken up with Nihat, İsmet treated Figen as if she were one of his own friends, made objective comments, and comforted her. Figen knew he genuinely wanted both of them to be happy, and she loved him sincerely too.

"Hello, my dear," İsmet answered the phone.

Figen talked. She talked and talked... She talked about how much she loved Nihat. She talked about how she missed him. She talked about how tired she was of breaking up. She talked about how she didn't understand why they couldn't be happy. İsmet listened to Figen without interrupting her once. When Figen finished, İsmet began to speak:

"Well then, my dear sister, if that's the case, why did you go around telling people that you're better off without Nihat?"

Figen was shocked. She had never said anything about being better off without Nihat in any of their breakups. Moreover, even if she had said it, which friend would dare to go and tell Nihat such a thing? She couldn't comprehend it.

"Could such a thing be possible, I didn't say anything like that to anyone," she managed to say.

"You know better who you told what or didn't tell, of course," said İsmet.

This answer didn't satisfy Figen.

"Tell me, İsmet, what's going on, I have no idea about any of this."

"Honestly, Figen, it's not my place to say."

"Mate, it's not your place, but you're throwing out something like that, and I have no idea what it's about, İsmet!"

"I'd better not say anything more, why don't you talk to Nihat."

"Okay, hold on, let me call him..."

She hung up. Her hands and feet were trembling. She talked about Nihat with everyone, but these conversations never contained anything negative; she only talked about how much she missed him, how this breakup was destroying her. It was impossible for someone to have told Nihat something negative.

She hurriedly found Nihat's name in her contacts. Although she let it ring for a long time, he didn't answer. She called once more. The phone didn't answer again. She stopped herself from calling back to back. No, Figen. No. Be different this time.

She put the phone on one of the shelves in her library. She was burning up inside. She kept going back and looking at the clock. Four minutes had passed. When she got out of the shower, only ten minutes had passed. Time wasn't moving.

With a towel around her, water dripping from her hair, she had just picked up the phone to message Nihat when she saw a message had come from Nihat:

"In a meeting, I'll call in an hour."

She breathed a deep sigh of relief. She didn't know how the hour would pass, but with the comfort of knowing she would talk to Nihat in an hour, she went back to the bathroom to dry her hair.

Be patient for an hour, Figen. It's hard for you, but be patient.

***

Figen was dressed, staring blankly at her phone screen, when the phone rang. It was Nihat.

"Nihat, how are you?"

"I'm fine, Figen, how are you?"

"Thanks. I'd like to talk about something, if possible."

"Go ahead, I'm listening, Figen."

"Can we talk face to face?"

"No, let's talk on the phone."

A great disappointment passed over her heart like a concrete levelling machine. But insisting wouldn't help; she knew that very well.

"I spoke to İsmet today, he said some things but I didn't understand, I insisted but he didn't explain, he said 'talk to Nihat'."

"I see."

"Will you tell me what happened?"

"Figen, forget it, it's past now. There's nothing to talk about."

"But it's a matter concerning me, apparently I'm being accused of talking behind your back, I want to know what happened."

"Figen, ask your mother about these things, not me."

It was as if boiling water had been poured over Figen's head. What did her mother have to do with any of this?

"Sorry, I don't understand?" said Figen.

"Talk to your mother, Figen, I have nothing to tell you."

"Okay," she said, hanging up.

Furiously, she called her mother. That day, her mother was supposed to pick up Mert Can from nursery and come home. She had just arrived at school. "Come home quickly, without dawdling, I'm going to kill you," she said, hanging up.

***

"I didn't say anything."

"Don't you lie to me, Mum, what did you say to Nihat, tell me quickly!

This argument lasted a full six hours. Aynur had called Nihat on a day she had argued with Figen and told him everything: who Figen saw when they were apart, how she saw them, everything in detail. Moreover, she had said that Figen hated Nihat, that Figen constantly said, "The day I fall in love with someone else, I'll kick Nihat out, he's long deserved such a breakup," and she had emphatically explained that if he didn't want to be cheated on like this, it would be better for him to leave Figen, that he deserved a good woman.

Nihat had gone mad upon hearing this and had punished Figen with the breakup.

Figen was foaming with anger; she had managed to put Mert Can to sleep with difficulty and was restraining herself from killing her mother. Figen was crying like a madwoman, screaming, swearing all the curses she knew. Figen was starting to become rigid with anger again. Her face was purple, her tears mixing with her snot, her snot with her drool. Mert Can was waking up from the noise, and her mother went and put the child back to sleep.

"Why, Mum, why?" she said when her mother returned.

"Why didn't you love me the way every mother loves her child, why couldn't you strive for my happiness, can't you see I can't be happy without your love, why are you driving me mad like this?" she said.

Aynur, however, looked at Figen with empty eyes, and instead of calming her down, provoked her further:

"Look at this state, look at this state, look at the insults you're hurling at your mother over some man."

Figen grabbed Aynur by the throat:

"Don't you understand, don't you understand that I can't breathe without Nihat, how could you go and talk like that!"

Aynur replied with insolence:

"So, is what I said a lie?"

It wasn't a lie. In moments of extreme anger and nervous breakdowns, Figen had said similar things. But these were all sentences uttered in anger. And even if they were true, what a mother should do for her child is not to go and tell these things to her lover, but to sweep them under the carpet. Figen felt betrayed on top of the pain of losing Nihat. At that moment, she couldn't decide which pain was worse. Was the pain of her mother stabbing her, breaking her, for the umpteenth time greater, or the pain of having lost Nihat dozens of times? She didn't know...

"Lies! Lies! What kind of mother are you, what kind of person are you!"

Figen had fallen to her knees, sobbing hysterically.

"Get up, get up, the child will wake up now, look at this pathetic state."

Figen leapt up from where she was. She grabbed Aynur by the collar.

"Look at me, that's enough, I'll kill you."

Aynur, with a smug smile on her face, widening her mouth, replied:

"This is what you deserve."

Figen once remembered, when she was very little, watching a train pass on a railway line, she had leaned her head too far over the tracks. The train had passed in front of her so fast, so hard, and so suddenly that the wind had taken her breath away, and its passing just inches from her face had stunned her. Then she had felt nauseous for an hour and couldn't recover.

Well, when her mother said, "This is what you deserve," she remembered that moment for a second. It had come to her so suddenly, so harshly, that she began to feel nauseous.

Only yellowish lights appeared before her eyes; she couldn't see anything clearly. When she started to see, her mother was lying on the floor covered in blood, and she was standing over her, a knife in her hand, drenched in blood.

"A child can live without a mother, but no child whose mother betrays them can live a normal life", she thought to herself, feeling relieved, lighter.

And that is exactly how they got from the beginning to the end.

THE BEGINNING

Aynur, 1975, Üsküdar

"Would you tell me, please, which way I ought to go from here?" Alice asked.

"That depends a good deal on where you want to get to," said the Cat.

"I don't much care where—" said Alice.

"Then it doesn't matter which way you go," said the Cat.

"—so long as I get somewhere," Alice added as an explanation.

"Oh, you're sure to do that," said the Cat, "if you only walk long enough."

Alice's Adventures in Wonderland

Fatoş hadn't gone to her cleaning job that day. Bedri hadn't been coming home for a while. The man who was her former, or rather still her legal, husband hadn't stopped his harassment; he kept circling the house. Fatoş had run away from home, leaving her lawful husband and two children behind for Bedri. Within a year, Aynur was born, and they had started living with Bedri.

Bedri was a womaniser, married to another woman, a father of four. Although Fatoş was aware of Bedri's womanising, she didn't speak up, hoping he wouldn't leave her.

Despite hiding their address very well and not appearing in public, her husband always managed to find them wherever they went, raiding the house and having Bedri beaten. Similarly, Fatoş's family also hated her, seeing the situation as a matter of honour.

Worn down by the beatings, Bedri had left the house and showed no signs of returning.

Fatoş was left alone with a small child, going out cleaning to make a living. She could neither reach Bedri nor ask her family for help.

That day, while cleaning the house, the doorbell rang. When she opened the door, feeling miserable, she found her brother and her husband facing her. As she prepared to scream, her eyes wide with fear, her husband punched her in the centre of her chest, knocking her to the ground.

They stormed in. After looking around, they locked the door from the inside. Her brother and husband dragged the woman on the floor inside. Aynur ran and hid under the divan.

They beat and beat the woman trying to get up from the floor. Fatoş gathered herself and stood up. She punched her brother, who was kicking her, with all her might.

She hit him right in the middle of his face so hard that blood spurted from his nose. A bystander might have almost seen Fatoş smile. It was as if it wasn't a reflex formed at that moment but a move planned for years. For that day on the construction site, because he always mocked her, because instead of protecting her and accepting her with her faults he joined this monster to harm her, because he drove the man she loved away, because her mother loved him more than her, and for many other grievances that didn't come to mind at that moment…

Only a few seconds passed between these thoughts crossing her mind and her doubling over from a burning sensation in her stomach. She felt a burning sensation again, and again. A sharp hatred was piercing through her body. Blood flowed like pus from the pierced places. When she brought her two hands to her stomach, she realised they were covered in blood. She had fallen to her knees, trying to regulate her breath. She had been stabbed twelve times; the area around her knees was a growing circle of blood. Before she fell face down, she only thought, "I could have been happier."

***

When Fatoş collapsed face down, the two men looked at each other in panic. The husband, took the knife from the brother whose hands were covered in blood, and threw it towards Fatoş lying on the ground. They ran out. Aynur was trembling with fear, unable to come out from under the divan due to the shock she had experienced. She stayed under the divan for about four hours. She had covered her face with her hands, afraid to look at her mother who was looking at her from under the hanging cover of the divan. When she was sure the men had left, she came out from under the divan. She stood by the head of her mother's corpse lying on the floor, looking silently at her mother. And that's how it all began.

> *Either I hid my madness very well,*
>
> *or*
>
> *you*
>
> *were too stupid*
>
> *to see that I was mad.*